MORE CHEERS FOR JESS LOUREY'S
MURDER-BY-MONTH MYSTERY SERIES

September Fair

★ "Once again, the very funny Lourey serves up a delicious dish of murder, mayhem, and merriment."—*Booklist* (starred review)

"Lively."—*Publishers Weekly*

"[A]n entirely engaging novel with pathos, plot twists, and quirky characters galore … Beautifully written and wickedly funny."
—Harley Jane Kozak, Agatha, Anthony, and Macavity Award-winning author of *A Date You Can't Refuse*

August Moon

★ "Hilarious, fast paced, and madcap."—*Booklist* (starred review)

"Another amusing tale set in the town full of over-the-top zanies who've endeared themselves to the engaging Mira."—*Kirkus Reviews*

"[A] hilarious, wonderfully funny cozy."—*Crimespree Magazine*

Knee High by the Fourth of July

Shortlisted for a 2008 Lefty Award from Left Coast Crime

Chosen as a September 2007 Killer Book by the Independent Mystery Booksellers Association (KillerBooks.org)

"Mira … is an amusing heroine in a town full of quirky characters."—*Kirkus Reviews*

"Lourey's rollicking good cozy planted me in the heat of a Minnesota summer for a laugh-out-loud mystery ride."—Leann Sweeney, author of the Yellow Rose Mystery series

June Bug

"The funny, earthy heroine of *June Bug* is sure to stumble her way into the hearts of readers everywhere. Don't miss this one—it's a hoot!"—William Kent Krueger, Anthony Award-winning author of the Cork O'Connor series

"Jess Lourey offers up a funny, well-written, engaging story… readers will thoroughly enjoy the well-paced ride."—Carl Brookins, author of *The Case of the Greedy Lawyers*

"Jess Lourey is a talented, witty, and clever writer."—Monica Ferris, author of the bestselling Needlecraft Mysteries

May Day

"All the ingredients for a successful small town cozy series are here…"—*Publishers Weekly*

"Lourey's debut has a likeable heroine and a surfeit of sass…"—*Kirkus Reviews*

"*May Day* is fresh, the characters quirky. Minnesota has many fine crime writers, and Jess Lourey has just entered their ranks!"—Ellen Hart, author of the Sophie Greenway and Jane Lawless Mystery series

OCTOBER
FEST

OCTOBER FEST

A Murder-By-Month Mystery

jess lourey

MIDNIGHT INK
WOODBURY, MINNESOTA

First Edition
First Printing, 2011

Book design and format by Donna Burch
Cover design by Ellen Lawson
Cover illustration © Carl Mazer
Editing by Connie Hill

Midnight Ink, an imprint of Llewellyn Worldwide Ltd.

Library of Congress Cataloging-in-Publication Data
Lourey, Jess, 1970–
  October fest / by Jess Lourey.—1st ed.
     p.   cm. — (A murder-by-month mystery ; #6)
  ISBN: 978-0-7387-2623-6
1. Minnesota—Fiction. 2. Murder—Investigation—Fiction. 3. Chick lit.
I. Title.
  PS3612.O833O37   2011
  813'.6—dc22   2010050642

Midnight Ink
Llewellyn Worldwide Ltd.
2143 Wooddale Drive
Woodbury, MN 55125-2989
www.midnightinkbooks.com

Printed in the United States of America

DEDICATION

To Terri Bischoff, without whom this book
would never have been written.

ONE

If I was a dog, I would have smelled the murder coming. I'd have caught its scent on the breeze, a hint of rotten death weaving through the chill fall air, lacing around the shedding trees, creeping over the light morning frost on mouse footsteps. Hunting me.

But I wasn't a dog. I was a thirty-year-old woman who hoped but did not believe that she could get a fair shake in life's casino of love, success, and self-acceptance. The tables felt decidedly stacked this morning even though the October sun sparkled, covering me like a blanket against the still-crisp air clinging to the low ground. Ron Sims, my boss at the *Battle Lake Recall*, had ordered me to cover the Octoberfest inaugural event—a political debate—which is why I was mincing my way across the high school football field on this chummy Saturday morning, the scent of rotting leaves in the air and my sweet new shoes cutting at my heels. I'd never attended Battle Lake's premier fall festival, but Sunny, the woman whose house I was sitting, had informed me it was a beer-soaked, polka-driven, sausage-and-potato-embracing celebration.

Frankly, it didn't sound wildly different than your average weekend in this part of the world.

My newspaper reporting gig didn't consume much of my time usually. Ron, who was the owner and editor-in-chief of the *Recall*, required a weekly food column and four full-spread articles a month, some of them investigative. In return, he paid me $25 a week and I had an outlet for my itchy curiosity. I wasn't blind to the slave wages, though, and channeled my resentment directly into the culinary column, which I'd renamed "Battle Lake Bites" when I took it over in May.

The column was Halloween-themed this entire month, and instead of simply rounding up recipes with spooky names, I'd gone whole hog. My week-one column had featured instructions for creating Haunted Head Cheese. The "cheese" in the title is a misnomer; the "head" is not. Ask a German. And last week I'd offered instructions on creating Bitter Blood Sausage. All meat sausage contains some blood, you say? Not a quarter cup per serving, intentionally added. For the upcoming column, I was debating between Three Fried Mice (turns out you need to marinate rodents in ethyl alcohol to kill the plague and whatnot before frying) and Fearsomely Frightening Fish Chili, which I thought some locals might actually enjoy. It called for fresh fish plus their "juice" (a term which made me giggle and then feel ill), a little dill, some kidney beans, diced onions and garlic, chili powder, and voila! Frightening.

Come to think of it, if I picked that nearly edible recipe over the freakier alternative, maybe Ron would assign me fewer early morning jobs. I wasn't a big follower of politics and figured this beat to be his punishment for dedicating the Bitter Blood Sausage column to him. Any dish that depends upon a delicate balance between cream, lard, and fresh pork blood is probably best left unascribed. I'd need to find a stealthier way to exercise my passive aggressiveness, I decided, as I neared the carnival-sized main tent with the red flag perched on top.

The main tent housed this morning's event, a public debate between the two lead candidates campaigning for Minnesota's 7th District congressional seat. Arnold Swydecker was running against the incumbent, Sarah Glokkmann. Glokkmann had gone to school just up the road from Battle Lake and was garnering a lot of national press for her habit of slamming her foot in her mouth. Last week, around a mouthful of lefse, she'd confided to a Daughters of Norway gathering that it was her firm belief that all immigrants should be shipped home, toot suite, so real Americans could reclaim their country. Local camera crews had been in attendance, and the footage went viral. Ron was hopeful that today I could scoop her saying something particularly incendiary and drive up newspaper sales. In the meantime, the election was three short weeks away, and the candidates were neck and neck in the polls. I may only be a transplant, but I knew this race was important to a lot of people.

I'd relocated to this tiny, west-central Minnesota burg this past March to watch my friend Sunny's place and dog so she could accompany her monobrowed lover to Alaska. She was Battle Lake born and raised, inheriting 200 acres of rolling heaven bordering a pristine lake on the edge of town when her parents died in a car accident. She'd returned to the property after high school, spending part of her inheritance to replace the rundown farmhouse with a double-wide. She'd been happy living on the land and waiting tables until she fell in love with Dean, a furry, silver-tongued salmon fisherman who was hitching through town on his way back to the Great White North. She bought his and hers plane tickets, made me promise to guard her possessions for the summer, and flew into the sunset.

I'd found a full-time job running the library after the head librarian disappeared under mysterious circumstances. I was shamefully unqualified for the job, but there'd been so many deadly upheavals since then that my lacking the necessary degree and experience had taken a back seat in terms of Battle Lake's priorities. The town was reeling from a rash of murders, far too many for such a beautiful little burg. I stumbled through my workdays, spending my off time lurking on librarian blogs and reading library science textbooks so I didn't make a full-dress fool of myself. I'd signed on to the part-time reporting gig to supplement my anemic city-issued library paycheck. Overall, I made enough money to pay my bills, dine out once a week, and every now and again squirrel away a few nuts into my Get Outta Dodge fund. Then summer had passed, and Sunny had decided she didn't want to leave Alaska around the same time I decided I didn't want to leave Battle Lake. I didn't know if it was a decision so much as a lack of options, but I wore it the same.

I entered the tent and was greeted by the smell of musty canvas and trampled grass. The structure housed at least 50 people, though the crowd seemed Lilliputian within the enormous tent, rows of cafeteria tables ready for tonight's blowout festival. Not With My Horse, a local band featuring my ex, had been fine-tuning their "polka fusion" music for a week. This included, I'd heard, the keyboard player acquiring some phat accordion skillz. The Rusty Nail would serve beer, and Stub's Dining and Saloon would be catering sausage, chicken schnitzel, fried potatoes, and their famously fresh and warm four-style bread rolls. My stomach growled thinking about it. I'd left the house this morning with only enough time to grab a peanut butter granola bar and a bad attitude.

I hadn't decided if I'd join tonight's festivities or not. Newly dry, I was feeling vulnerable to be exposing myself to so much easy liquor. I decided to decide later and studied the gathered audience before choosing a prime spot. Only one person did I recognize as a local at a glance: Tanya Ingebretson, wife to the richest man in Battle Lake, on every city committee, in charge of every church function, and shallow as a grave. She'd been trying to get me fired from the library since I'd taken over, saying I lacked the credentials and didn't reflect the values of the town. The fact that she was right didn't make me like her any more. It didn't surprise me that she'd expand her political pie-fingering to the national level.

I settled in a folding chair toward the back of the crowd, noticing that to my left and right, sharply-dressed reporters clacked away on their tiny handhelds, press passes dangling at their neck. Since I'd forgotten my press pass, I settled for yanking out my writing utensil and pad of paper to make like I was texting someone with my pencil, which, it turns out, looked just like I was taking notes. Which I was.

Murmurs of conversation ran through those gathered, but most of us stared quietly toward the stage, waiting for the show to start. We were in luck. On the makeshift platform, a woman in an elegant green pantsuit separated herself from a throng of people and approached an '80s-era, large-bulbed microphone perched on a silver stick. She cleared her throat and shoved her shoulder-length red hair behind her ear in a self-conscious gesture. She appeared about my age, but classy.

"Hello, and thank you for coming. My name is Grace Swinton, and I'm Representative Glokkmann's assistant." Her voice was high and clear. "I'm afraid the debate is running late due to a … scheduling conflict, but we should be ready to roll in under a half an hour."

A hot whisper ran through the audience. The camera crews on the fringe sighed and put down their heavy-looking equipment, and the reporter nearest me said to no one in particular, "I bet I know what that conflict is."

"Really?" I swiveled toward him. "What?"

He glanced at my scruffy jeans, t-shirt under a lined jean jacket, and hair in a pony tail. I gathered it required some effort to take me seriously, but he was a champ, holding his thumb and pinky out and putting them up to his mouth in a drinking motion.

I was familiar with the gesture for "drinking problem." Boy was I. And I loved the dirt. Maybe this debate wouldn't be boring after all. "One of the candidates?"

My eagerness must have repelled him. He shrugged and turned his attention to the man to his right. I tried to eavesdrop, but they were clearly friends, their heads in close as they engaged in animated but quiet conversation. Having worn out my welcome I stood, planning to take the subtle route and sidle toward the stage to sniff out who reeked of whiskey and mouthwash. The tippler had to be one of the speakers to put the debate on hold, but which one? I was woefully unfamiliar with the facts of either. If I owned a handheld, I could probably look up the info right here. Instead, I went old school, strolling over to a woman with Asian features—Korean lineage if I had to guess—perched near the edge of the stage. She was not clearly affiliated with the press or the debaters.

"Nice day," I said, glancing around the tent.

She studied me intently for a second and then looked away, like a hawk deciding I wasn't worth the flight. I put her at mid to late twenties, her skin clear and her features striking. She was dressed casually, but expensive casual in high-end jeans and a well-cut blazer.

I tried again. "You on one of the campaigns?"

Still nothing.

"Ever been to Battle Lake before?" The woman rolled her eyes so loud I could hear it. I switched to the direct route. "Look, I have to cover this debate because my editor wants to punish me. I wanna know if it's worth my time to hang out for something that might never happen. I hear one of the candidates is, you know." I made the same sign for "in the bottle" that the reporter had and felt like a thief for doing it.

I'd hit a nerve. "The debate'll happen," she said. "Queen Glokkmann never misses an opportunity for an audience."

From her mouth to God's ears, because a flurry of activity materialized on the stage. The waiting camera crews hoisted their equipment onto their shoulders and reporters slipped their handhelds into their pockets and leaned toward the stage. "Thanks," I said, grabbing an empty chair in the front row between two strangers too polite to sit next to each other.

Once seated, I observed that the dark-haired woman was no longer skulking on the sidelines. A security guard had replaced her, a transparent cord coiling out from an earpiece to a chunk of plastic on his shoulder. A long table was slid to the front of the stage, and two stubby cordless microphones were plunked on it, one next to the "Representative Sarah Glokkmann" placard and the other next to the "Arnold Swydecker" placard. A short blonde woman I recognized as a waitress from Stub's scurried out with a pitcher of water and two glasses, taking a shy moment to glance out at the audience from the star's perspective.

"This looks like it's gonna happen," I whispered to the woman on my left, who had a tape recorder in hand. She smiled and nodded without peeling her eyes off the stage.

I leaned toward the older gentleman on my right. He sported a cookie duster mustache and a press pass indicating he worked for the

Fergus Falls Register. "Hey, you know which of the two candidates is the biggest drunk?" He pursed his lips and dismissively shook his head without glancing away from the stage, either.

I followed their gaze. The woman who had earlier made the debate delay announcement, Grace something or the other, re-emerged looking frazzled, making me like her infinitely more.

"Thank you for your patience!" She really seemed to mean it. "On behalf of Representative Sarah Glokkmann, I'd like to thank you all for coming. The values and concerns of rural Minnesota are our values and concerns. We look forward to serving the state for another two years and beyond."

She motioned toward the back of the stage where a makeshift curtain had been erected, gesturing for someone to step forward. Nobody did. She motioned again and waited an uncomfortable minute before giving up. "And Mr. Swydecker needs no introduction at all. So, let's begin the debate. Both candidates have prepared a statement that they will read. Then, they will each have two minutes to answer questions submitted by District 7 voters. Finally, we will take questions from the media." She smiled at us to indicate that whatever we wanted to ask would be A-okay.

"With no further ado, let the debates begin!" She shoved the microphone into the crook of her arm and clapped, walking backward so as not to block the view of the candidates.

Sarah Glokkmann arrived at the edge of the stage first, modeling sandy brown Lego-lady hair, thick orange make-up that probably looked great on TV, and an ill-fitting coral sports jacket over a matching skirt. Arnold Swydecker shambled behind her looking like he'd been trotted out of a fifth grade band room where he'd been boring kids since the late seventies, all gray comb-over and hunched back from peering too closely at the sheet music for "Another One Bites the Dust." Both had the makings of a career drinker, as far as I could tell.

They waved at the live audience and the cameras before claiming their seats. Glokkmann spoke first. She couldn't be older than her mid-forties despite the dowdy clothes. She was poised, I'd give her that, though if I wasn't mistaken, she had a slight tremor in her left hand. "Thank you for coming, Battle Lake!" She fist-pumped the air, effectively hiding the wobble. Her cadre on stage left hooted, drawing the attention of the cameras. On the news, it'd look like there was a whole cheering section.

"I've served you faithfully for six years, and I'm willing to continue my work for as long as you'll have me. Now, my opponent over here will tell you that I haven't done enough, but I'd like to remind him of the thirteen bills I've been involved with since elected to office."

Someone behind me snorted loudly. I snuck a glance and noted that it was the reporter who'd first mentioned a drinking problem. Drat. I shouldn't have been so desperate with him.

The snort, however, did not break Glokkmann's stride. She smiled winningly at the audience, revealing two dimples as deep as oil wells. Her hands were clasped tightly in front of her. "What is important to me is what's important to you. Increased money in your wallets. Healthier communities. Stronger families. More jobs."

It occurred to me that I should be writing this down, but I didn't see how she could be any vaguer short of saying, "I like good stuff!" She continued dishing out the pabulum for another ten minutes before tossing a gracious nod to Swydecker, who was as sincere as he was boring. In a mumbling, shuffling voice, he explained how his thirty years in the education system (I knew it!) taught him the value of strong public schools and well-funded libraries, the benefit to communities if families had access to living wages and health benefits, and the importance of preserving the environment for future generations by making unpopular decisions now. He did not have a hooting section, not even a small one. In fact, I wouldn't have noticed when he stopped talking except he and the Representative took their seats.

The debate followed a pattern after that: Grace would read a question, which didn't seem fair as we knew whose team she was on. Glokkmann would answer it with a chirpy ball of nothing, and then Swydecker would respond in a specific and stultifying way before being cut off for running over his time limit. The only alteration to this pattern was in who spoke first. I didn't want to embarrass myself by nodding off and so instead closed one eye and pretended to squish the tiny heads of the people on stage.

Before I knew it, it was time for questions from the audience. I raised my hand not because I had something to ask but because I needed to reassure myself I was awake. Thankfully I wasn't called on. Instead, the blonde woman to my left got her chance. "Representative Glokkmann, there's rumors that you're considering throwing your hat into the governor ring. Is it true?"

The Representative smiled brightly. "Lila, right now my priority is serving the state in the position they've elected me to. I have no other political ambitions at this time. If that changes, my family will be the first to know, and you'll be the second." The audience laughed politely, and Glokkmann winked in Lila's direction.

Someone behind me was called on next. He stood. "Mr. Swydecker, what are your feelings on the current war?"

Swydecker appeared somber and thoughtful, which apparently was the debate equivalent of showing your throat in a dog fight. "Depends on what day you ask, doesn't it Arnie?" Glokkmann interrupted, smiling as she sliced. "But I'm always on the side of the troops and America."

Handy, I thought, settling in for a twenty-minute playground fight with Glokkmann playing the role of lunch-stealer. I was about to pack it up when the reporter who'd tipped me on the tippler was finally called on. Grace seemed to have been deliberately avoiding acknowledging him because he'd had his hand up since before the official audience Q & A period and had been holding it impatiently aloft since.

"Yes, Bob Webber, right?" Grace said icily. "What newspaper are you with again?"

"I have a blog, actually, Ms. Swinton, but I believe you know that," he said, standing. "It's called *The Body Politic*. My question is for Representative Glokkmann." He cleared his throat, and I noticed that the arms of his sport coat were a little short, the front shiny from wear. He looked vulnerable standing there, like a kid owning only hand-me-downs dressing his best for a big speech. "Ma'am, the only bill you have successfully sponsored in your three terms in the legislature is House Resolution 1294, which calls for the designation of the month of September as 'National Moebius Syndrome Awareness Month.' Of the twelve other bills you've co-sponsored, six are directly related to opening up national lands to gas and oil exploration, development, and production. Two are aimed at killing the health-care bill so insurance companies rather than doctors get to decide what health care we receive, while your husband coincidentally owns an insurance company. Do you have any ethical qualms about doing little else in Congress other than using your position to line the pockets of the oil industry and your family?"

Glokkmann held her smile, though it cracked a little at each corner. "Bob, tell me what you know about Moebius Syndrome." Both hands were definitely shaking now.

"That's not my question, ma'am."

11

"I'll tell you what I know. I know it's an unfair disease that affects thousands, and through awareness and support, we can make a difference in the lives of children who face this tremendous hurdle. You're telling me that advocating for those who can't advocate for themselves is 'doing little'?"

I always thought I had a gift for deflection, the pretty little sister of lying, but this lady was a pro. I craned my head fully so I could watch Webber's reaction. His cheeks flushed, and he was shifting his weight from one foot to another. He knew he couldn't pursue his line of questioning without looking coldhearted. Score one for the Lego-haired Lady. He sat down abruptly, and I turned back in time to see her smile triumphantly, her hands once again clasped in front of her.

Grace stepped in to announce the debate successful, and at an end. The candidates moved to the edge of the stage and shook hands while worker ants sprang up to clear the stage and prepare it for the night's festivities. I wove through the crowd to reach Bob the blogger and was nearly there when a commotion erupted at the rear of the tent. A group of six or seven people marched in, all of them carrying protest signs. The posters I could read proclaimed health care a right and not a privilege, and the sign holders were chanting angrily, demanding an audience with Glokkmann and Swydecker.

I toggled to get a closer look, but so did all the other reporters and the camera crews, causing a bottleneck. Moving to the side instead of fighting forward, I was able to catch a glimpse of the dark-haired woman who'd assured me "Queen Glokkmann" would not miss a debate slide into the tent through the same opening as the protestors, a smirk on her face. She strode toward the stage and took a post where she could watch both the candidates and the sign holders. Swydecker was watching the sign holders with interest. Glokkmann, on the other hand, was high-tailing it toward an exit. The security guard material-ized alongside the protestors.

I wished I had a chance to see how it all turned out, but I had to open up the library. I scribbled Bob the blogger's name in my note-book, wondering if his last name was spelled with one or two b's, and set off to start my shift. Of course, if I was a dog, I'd have bolted straight out of town, my hackles razor-sharp. The murder had never been closer, butcher and victim sharing the same tent air.

TWO

THE BATTLE LAKE PUBLIC Library had served as my refuge since I'd arrived in town, an oasis of comforting words, leafy plants in the windows, a place for everything and everything in its place. I let myself in and grabbed the stack from the Book Return bin on my way to fire up the front desk computer. I loved having a peephole into what Battle Lake read. Today's load featured *Artificial Intelligence for Dummies* with several pages dog-eared, a handful of romance novels, two books on training boxers (the dog, not the fighter), four hardcover bestsellers, all of which I had a waiting list for, and a Thai cookbook with a gorgeous cover photo of slivered pork in cilantro broth alongside fresh spring rolls and a tiny pot of peanut sauce. I was so busy slavering over the culinary possibilities that I didn't notice the shadow on the other side of the door. I almost jumped over my hair when the greeting bells jingled.

"Oh! We don't open for another thirty minutes." I said, turning. I was all set to explain the library's limited weekend hours to whomever was entering when my glance connected with beautiful eyes so profoundly blue that I swear clouds floated in his eyelashes. "Johnny!" My exclamation was half joy, half fear, a mix that comes easily to both cult members and women too stupid to fall in love with the right guy.

"Hey, Mir. Were you covering the debate this morning?" He smiled tentatively, and the sight of his full lips moving slowly over straight white teeth gave me a shiver in my happy place. Johnny and I had been dancing an awkward salsa the past few months, with him dating someone and then single, moving closer until I pushed him away, him acceding until I pulled him closer. This embarrassing hustle was made worse by the fact that his lean, muscled beauty dorkified me immediately, garbling my words and propelling me to say stupid, sarcastic stuff to cover my unease. Johnny had persisted, however, and we'd both been rewarded with a magnificent, earth-shaking, kiss-on-a-stick at the State Fair a few weeks back. Not wanting to mess up my dream image of him with reality, or give him a chance to not like me by getting to know me, I'd studiously avoided him since the spectacular, love-and-rockets joining of our lips. Until this moment.

"Johnny!" That was it. That was my conversational tour de force.

He smiled wider and shoved his hands into his jean pockets, which were slung low on his hips. During the summer, he worked at Swedberg Nursery, and he still had a residual tan from a season spent outdoors. His shaggy blonde hair hung in his face, thick as a book and curling around his neck. He was dressed in the male version of my outfit—fleece-lined brown corduroy jacket, white T-shirt, and rough blue jeans. "Hope I'm not bothering you. You haven't returned my calls. Everything okay?"

"Yeah. Sure. You know how it is." Why was I blushing?

He stepped in quickly and held me before I could protest. He smelled like cinnamon toothpaste and fresh air. "I've missed you."

He caught me off guard, overriding my defense mechanisms and the speech center in my brain. I could feel his lean hips pressing against my stomach, his sculpted chest against mine. Dang, he felt good. "Hard as a board," I whispered.

"What?" He asked, pulling away.

"Good lord! I mean … power cord. I need a new power cord for the library. Just, you know, going over my shopping list. Didn't know I'd said it out loud." I forced a grin, my face bright enough to read by.

His smile was puzzled. "I'm sure the hardware store has some on hand. I'll check for you. I need to stop by there today, anyhow. What's the power cord for?"

My blood was still too far south to do my brain any good. "Power," I said.

He nodded and changed the subject, stepping back another hair. "I just came from the Senior Sunset. Mrs. Berns says 'hi.'"

The mention of Mrs. Berns' name should have set my danger danger radar off, but it, too, was enthralled by the magnificence that was Johnny. I'd met Mrs. Berns shortly after arriving in Battle Lake. She'd marched up to me and informed me that she was my new assistant librarian. After witnessing my second corpse in sixty days, I wasn't in a state of mind to argue the finer points of experience or pay, or the fact that I didn't need an assistant. She'd shouldered her way into the Battle Lake Library just like she'd shouldered her way into my life, infuriating me, saving my life, and making me look forward to my eighties. Oh yeah. Mrs. Berns turned eighty-seven last week. "Really? How's she doing?"

He ran his hands through his hair. "The usual, mostly. She said she's hardly seen you since the State Fair, either."

I grimaced at the emphasis on "either." Johnny I'd been avoiding on purpose, but Mrs. Berns was my best friend. I had been self-involved the past couple weeks, fall-cleaning my garden, prepping the house for winter by installing clear plastic over the windows and caulking drafty cracks, and catching up on my reading. Since Mrs. Berns, whose library schedule was whimsical during the best of times, hadn't seen fit to show up for work since the summer crowds had fled town, our paths hadn't crossed. "I'll have to stop by."

"You should." He rocked a little on his feet. "She's taking a class at Alex Tech. Oh, and she mentioned something about her son being in town."

"The one who put her in the home?" I became aware that Johnny was feeling awkward, his body not fitting him quite right. Usually I was the artless one in this pairing. Was it something I'd said? I quickly ran through our five-minute interaction. Nah. I was good.

"I think so. She didn't want to talk about it much."

"Sounds like her. Now I *really* need to stop by. Maybe over my lunch hour." His fidgeting escalated. "Is everything okay?"

He nodded, suddenly tongue-tied, looking embarrassed for no reason I could fathom. I wondered if he was wrestling with some internal body function. I knew how that could take its conversational toll. Clueless as to how to handle being the suaver of the two of us, I angled away and pretended to organize the pile of returned books I'd gathered from the return bin. I felt like a dumb monkey shuffling and then reshuffling eleven books, but I wanted to give Johnny a chance to compose himself without me looking at him.

I stuck with it, waiting for Johnny to retake the reins, but next thing I knew, the front door chimed and he was gone, no more words spoken. I was alone in the library with the books, my accumulated baggage, and a crisp ivory envelope Johnny had left on the counter top, "Mira James" scrawled on the front in a masculine stroke.

THREE

My first sleepover with a guy didn't transpire until I was living on my own in the Cities at the sagacious age of eighteen. I was toxic property in my hometown of Paynesville, given my dad's shameful death. I saw no reason to complain—everyone has their knot to unravel in this life—but I'd spent my first sixteen years on this earth with an alcoholic father and an enabling mom. He put an end to half of that equation when he slithered behind the wheel with most of a liter of vodka gurgling in his belly. He took the occupants of another vehicle down with him, head on.

You can probably guess what being the daughter of a manslaughterer does to an already awkward teenaged girl, especially in Smalltown, Minnesota. I beat cheeks to Minneapolis as soon as I graduated and spent the next ten or so years sitting in on enough English classes to earn a bachelor's degree and drinking too many vodka and diet Cokes. It was a fear of ending up like my father that had driven me to housesit for Sunny, which was ironic because it turned out that in this west-central Minnesota oasis, alcohol was as necessary to a night out as shoes.

But before that, in high school I felt lucky to have a few girlfriends, forget dating a boy. By the time I escaped the constricting environment of Paynesville and made it into the Big World, my virginity had grown heavy, a white purse that you loved until you found out everyone else thought it was dumb. Probably I should have hung onto my purse—fashion is cyclical—rather than open it for Ben, my first official boyfriend.

He was a regular at Perfume River, the Vietnamese restaurant where I waited tables, a black-haired loner who asked me out via a note on the back of his bill for imperial beef with fried rice. Turned out he was in a band, which in Minneapolis at that time was like saying he had two hands. We hung out together in various bars for a few weeks, me with a fake ID and him monologuing about the raw originality of his music, until The Night. I hope I'm not breaking the virgin's covenant by revealing that the pleasure of the first time fell somewhere between a swimsuit wedgie and an off-trail bike ride, lasting approximately as long as the former.

Ben would never know what a gift he'd received. We broke up the next morning without ever really talking about it and proceeded in true Midwest fashion: we forgot we knew each other. I felt a little bad that he had to find a new restaurant to hang out in, but such is the price of a doomed relationship. I'd been with a handful of men since then, and though I was far from pro, I thought I'd seen enough to know when a guy asking me on a date really wanted to get to know me versus wanted to stick a toy surprise in my cereal box. That's why I was so puzzled by Johnny's letter.

Inside the envelope was a handwritten invitation requesting my presence at the Big Chief Motor Lodge this evening at nine p.m. in room 20. The Big Chief was the newest business in the growing town, opening its doors to the community last week. It sat on a key location one hundred feet from the shore of West Battle Lake, within eyeshot of Chief Wenonga, the glorious fiberglass statue that graced the perimeter of the town as well as my dreams. The statue was the gold standard of political incorrectness, but whenever I looked at it, I got all swoony and my heart skipped a beat. The statue was fashioned after the actual Chief Wenonga, an Ojibwe warrior. A hundred and some years ago he'd led the charge against the Dakota, another proud tribe who'd put down roots in this area.

History remembered Chief Wenonga as a gifted leader and fighter. Battle Lake, however, erected him as a stereotypical Old West Indian with full feather headdress snaking down his back, inky eyes and proud nose on a face slashed with war paint, adorned with leather pants and moccasins, an erect tomahawk in the left hand suggesting glorious things. My mind may never have gone there if the Chief statue wasn't also shirtless, the star Chippendale Dancer of the fiberglass world. Plus, he was emotionally distant, which up until Johnny, had been the kind of guy I was attracted to.

Ah, Johnny. Open and kind, he liked to garden, had a degree in biology from the University of Minnesota, and he was taking care of his sick mother during the day and rocking out as the lead singer of a popular band at night. He was perfect, and therefore all wrong for me. So why was he making this low-class move of asking me to meet in a hotel, and why put it on a written invitation suggesting I "dress casually?" That sounded completely unlike him. But, I had a pretty good idea who it *did* sound like.

———

The Senior Sunset is maple-lined walks with commemorative benches on the outside, institutional rooms with locked doors and paintings of pastel pastiche on the inside. From what I gathered, before Mrs. Berns had arrived, most of the clients at the Sunset spent their time watching TV or moaning for someone to brush their hair. Now, they giggled in corners as they passed black market copies of *GQ* and *Mademoiselle*, played cards for money, and hatched plans for afterhours slumber parties. Instead of following the gray road to their deaths, they pressed against the confinement of the home to squeeze bootlegged joy, the best kind, out of their final years. And it was all because of Mrs. Berns, who had followed society's rules for eighty years before deciding it was finally time to live by her own. And society always hates a deviant when it isn't invited to the party.

According to local gossip, she'd arrived in the area in the 1920s filling the typical Minnesota farmwife role, raising seven kids during the Depression, taking in extra sewing to make ends meet, hardworking and responsible every minute of the day. She hadn't slowed down even after the kids moved out and her husband's dairy farm started turning a profit, working dawn 'til sundown canning, mending, cleaning, and helping with chores. Her husband had been a solid man, no great romantic but a stable Swedish farmer who paid the bills and didn't yell at his wife. Mrs. Berns had completely fulfilled her hausfrau duties right up until her husband's death by heart attack a decade ago.

Legend had it, that's when Mrs. Berns underwent The Change. Her husband's body was barely cold when she put the farm on the market and moved to town. With a population under eight hundred in the winter and more bars than churches, you'd think Battle Lake would have welcomed its newest resident, but her sudden penchant for going braless combined with her willingness to say whatever was on her mind didn't go over well with the more conservative members of the community. When Conrad, her oldest son, got word of his sweet mother's out-of-character behavior, and specifically her newspaper-documented fistfight at the Rusty Nail over a man of questionable reputation ("Granny Goes Gonzo"), he promptly checked her into the Senior Sunset on threat of getting her declared mentally incompetent if she didn't comply.

On the surface, she bowed to his command. Behind the scenes, though, Mrs. Berns got right down to the business of circumventing the rules of the nursing home, sneaking out after hours to do as she pleased. Before long, she was the don of a profitable black market operation fencing cigarettes, airplane-sized bottles of liquor, and Tom Jones posters to those on the inside. After a near mutiny when he tried to crack the whip against these illicit antics, the director of the Senior Sunset chose to turn a blind eye to Mrs. Berns' behavior on her word there would be no more public brawling.

Mrs. Berns likely had her fingers crossed when she made that agreement. That's about when I met her, all fluffy-haired, bobby-socked, capgun-toting (don't ask), four-feet-eleven inches of her. Since then she'd taught me how to dirty dance, defend myself using moves not widely practiced outside of a pig-castrating shed, and live without regret. To be honest, I was still working on that last one. But as much as I loved her, she had a mischievous streak as wide as the Mississippi, and I smelled her fingerprints all over Johnny's invitation.

I signed in at the front desk. My lunch break was prime visiting hours and the check-in sheet was almost full. I smiled nervously at the nurse behind the desk, concealing the cloth bag I was carrying behind my back. It contained the secret to prying the truth out of Mrs. Berns: dark chocolate and a miniature bottle of red wine. I still couldn't wrap my head around the fact that nursing home residents were not officially allowed liquor, which was the crime of the century as far as I was concerned. My visiting privileges would be revoked indefinitely if I got caught with it, but it was a risk I was willing to take to get the Oracle to speak.

I wasn't sneaking toward Mrs. Berns' room, but I did stop when I heard the whispering inside. Followed by a giggle. That's when I noticed the cross-stitched, "Bless this Home" circle hanging off the doorknob, the signal that if this was a van, it'd be rocking so don't bother to come knocking. Glancing at the clock on the wall, I realized I didn't have time to wait. Buying the chocolate and wine had eaten up almost half an hour, and I needed to reopen the library at one o'clock. I knocked at the door, delicately and with more than a little fear.

The giggling stopped. "You knock like a girl." This was followed by a rustle of fabric and light footsteps. "This better be an emergency," she said on the other side of the door.

Her orange-shaded head popped out looking inconvenienced.

"Hi, Mrs. Berns."

"I made him write the invitation, it's a surprise so I can't tell you more, and it's not what you think." And she slammed the door in my face.

She must have a steamy number in her room or she wouldn't have passed up an opportunity to make me squirm, but curiosity was the one vice I consistently entertained. I knocked again, firmly.

"That's better, but it still doesn't get you in."

I turned the knob and stepped inside.

"*That'll* get you in," she said. And next to her, on her double GoldenRest Adjustable bed, was the *Fergus Falls Register* reporter with the soup-strainer mustache who'd sneered at me in the big tent earlier today. Small world. He didn't stand at my entrance, and Mrs. Berns didn't introduce him.

"I need to talk to you."

"I presume you do," she said, employing a slight British accent to mock my serious tone.

"It's really important."

She dropped the accent. "It's not about Johnny?"

"Well ..."

"Ach." She turned to the man lounging on her bed. "Bernard, I need to talk to Mira. Shouldn't take more'n a minute."

I stepped to the side so he could exit and leave us to our conversation, but he just loafed deeper into the bed, cranking the sound on the Discovery Channel, which was airing a show about the ancient mysteries of the Maya.

"I'll take a cherry cola while you're out," he said. "Not the barbaric kind. Thanks."

I wrinkled my nose at Mrs. Berns, but she shooed me out without making eye contact. In the hall, I asked, "Since when do you let someone kick you out of your own room? And what exactly is 'barbaric' soda?" That's when I noticed that she was wearing creepily traditional grandmother clothes: a Branson T-shirt sent to her by one of her kids which she'd used as a dust rag until recently, elastic-waisted slacks sans her low-slung holster, and fuzzy slippers. She looked, well, old.

"He means 'generic,' and I needed to go to the cafeteria, anyways," she said.

"Stop." I grabbed her hand and rotated her toward me. "I'm sorry I haven't been visiting regularly the last couple weeks. I've dropped the ball. I miss you. Now what is up with these clothes and that guy?"

The uncensored Mrs. Berns broke through the grandma garments. "You didn't drop nuthin', and frankly, I haven't missed that mopey need-to-get-laid look in your eyes. I've got to appear professional for a little while, is all."

"Why?"

"Can't tell you."

"Is it because your son is around? Johnny told me."

"He's a girl for gossiping. And it's none of your business."

I knit my brows. "Since when?"

"Since you should be busy worrying about whether or not you need to shave your legs for tonight." She cackled at the expression on my face.

I didn't want to get off topic that easily, but there was no point in pretending I wasn't outgunned. I sighed. "Do I?"

"When it comes to being ready for lovin', I think the Boy Scouts got it right: always be prepared."

"I don't think that's what they were referring to."

"Nevertheless."

I crossed my arms. "You're not going to tell me anything more, are you?"

She changed the subject as gracefully as a fish flew. "Nice T-shirt. Is that new?"

"Thank you, and no." I blew out angry and drew in happy. It sounded like an asthma attack. "When're you coming back to the library?"

"Don't know that I am. Come here. I've got something to show you." She detoured into the Sunset's communications center, which she'd raised local money to outfit. It housed three desktop computers with word processing, scrapbooking, and desktop publishing software on each, plus a color printer, a fax, a scanner, and a copier. She'd talked me and a handful of others into teaching basic classes on using e-mail

25

and "spoofing the net" as she called it, and now most of the residents were more computer-proficient than me.

All three work stations were empty, so she plopped into the nearest chair and pulled me next to her. Clickety-clack, and she pointed proudly at the screen.

"What am I looking at?" I asked.

"My registration. Check out the evidence of Alexandria Technical College's newest student."

"Johnny mentioned that. Good for you!"

"Jesus, he's weak. You sure you wouldn't rather sleep with a real man? Whoops, didn't mean to give anything away. Anyhow, I'm going to earn a degree in Fashion Management. The college started an Elder School this fall, and they offer new online classes every four weeks. I could have my degree within a year."

I leaned in closer to the screen and squinted to read the tiny black words. "You're registered for one class, and it's Human Sexuality. How does that connect to Fashion Management?"

"Only elective available this late in the game. Class starts Monday."

I curled my lip doubtfully. "What could they possibly teach you that you don't already know?"

She clicked again, and the syllabus popped up. "Looks like we'll be discussing our genitalia, sexual scripts whatever the moon those are, something called fellatio"—she pronounced it with a hard "t," no pun intended—"sexual positions…"

"Stop!" I had a lifetime membership in the club of girls who chose to believe Olivia Newton John's "Let's Get Physical" was about the benefits of aerobic workouts. I liked having sex; I just didn't like talking about it. "I get the picture."

"Besides, it'll be a great way to expand my horizons, get to know people on a new social landscape."

"That's not a social landscape, that's a mattress with textbooks," I said, and then caught myself. I believed in the power of education. Plus, I did not want to witness her in granny pants again. What better way to kickstart the old Mrs. Berns than by putting her in an environment where she could, nay, where she'd be *required* to talk about copulation and hang out with young people? She'd have her own religion started before midterm. "I think it's wonderful. I'm proud of you."

"Don't patronize me," she said. "And what chickenshit Johnny Leeson question do you have, anyhow?"

She jarred me back to the dilemma that had brought me. She'd already admitted to making him send the invitation, so I cut to the chase. "Why did Johnny let you talk him into the invitation? He's usually much more sensible. What does he want?"

"Holy Mary, girl, do you want to audit the class? I'm sure they have diagrams."

I blushed, my head spinning from her runaround. "So that's it? He just wants to get in my pants?"

"Ah, no, he's too nice a boy for that, dangit. You'll have to go yourself to find out what it is he's after."

"A hint?"

"Look to the boy scouts."

Rich words of wisdom from my love mentor, the woman who saw more action in her eighties than I'd seen in my entire thirty years on the planet. I squelched the urge to pinch her and instead gave her a hug.

———

My workday passed quickly but not particularly pleasantly as I ran through all the potential scenarios for the evening. I could bail, and

Johnny would never want to see me again. I could go to the motel, and Johnny would never want to see me again. Or, he wasn't who I thought he was at all and had some weird night of sex in mind. Or I did know him and he was going to ask for a commitment from me, some sort of official categorizing of our relationship. Agh. None of the options were good. I was so wound up when I closed the library and pulled into my driveway that even the sight of Luna bounding out to greet me didn't cheer me up. Nor did the saucy disdain directed at me by calico cat, Tiger Pop.

"Hi, babies," I said, climbing out of the car. The fall air was brisk but not frosty, saturated with the earthy smell of leaves turning and far off, someone burning wood. I clutched my jacket tighter, staring down the sloping, brown front lawn to the big red barn and fenced pasture that used to hold horses when Sunny lived here as a child. On the other side was the sparkling blue-gray of Whiskey Lake. This spot was idyllic, the house and outbuildings nestled amongst wild acres of golden-grassed prairie, rolling hills, and hardwood forests. Except for the smell of wood smoke, I could have been the only person in the universe. I dragged in a deep breath, momentarily refreshed.

Dog and cat followed me into the house where I rinsed out their water dishes and poured a fresh drink along with kibbles for the dog and pebble food for the kitty.

"How was your day? Were you good to each other?" Luna looked at me hopefully, like if she played her cards right I might make her as smart as a cat for a day. Tiger Pop ignored us both. I scratched them until one rolled over in ecstasy and the other purred against his will.

Animals sated, I cobbled together some vegetable soup to settle my sour stomach. I still hadn't made up my mind whether or not I was going to the motel tonight, and the indecision was making me queasy.

Crap. Who was I kidding? I'd made up my mind the minute I'd received the invitation. If only I was one of those women for whom good sense won out over inquisitiveness. Or, let's face it, for whom dead bodies didn't pile up like unwashed clothes. It occurred to me, then, that I hadn't seen a dead body since the State Fair. Maybe October would be my first corpse-free month since May, I thought hopefully. If I'd known I was less than twelve hours shy of ending that good luck streak in a most gruesome fashion, I wouldn't have bothered shaving.

FOUR

You're stupid, you're stupid, you're stupid, I told myself as my Toyota hugged the corner into town, spraying gravel. When I was six years old, my mother took me to see a movie in St. Cloud, the closest town with a theater. I don't remember where my dad was; probably my mom was trying to get us out of the house and away from him for a few hours. It was my first big screen experience: a remastered release of *Bambi*. The theater had also been updated, an old 1920s burlesque hall regilded, repainted, and recurtained to host modern film. I begged for seats in the balcony and was hypnotized when the theater went dark and the music came on, vibrating the chairs. Words appeared on the screen, followed by magical animation. We didn't even own a television at the time, so this was heady stuff.

For a while. Then, I spotted a group of boys a few years older than me on the main floor below giggling and passing something between them. I slid away from my mother—poor thing probably needed her own break—and over to the edge of the balcony. I could see that what they were passing was shiny, catching the glint when the screen went bright. Was it a knife? A metal bottle for drinking out of, like my dad had? A decoder ring? I couldn't quite make it out through the intricately patterned wrought iron barrier. Lucky thing there was a hole just big enough to squeeze my head through, if I wiggled and pushed. So I did, and to my great satisfaction, I saw that they were passing candy back and forth, a mother lode of U-No bars. I smiled—they'd snuck those in. I knew this because I'd begged my mom to buy me a Caravelle bar and I would have begged her to buy me a U-No bar instead if they'd sold them—and I kept smiling even as my horrified mother realized first that I was no longer seated next to her and second, that my head was wedged in the wrought iron tighter than Excalibur in the stone. It took two firefighters, a tub of Noxema, and a lot of elbow, neck, and ear grease to free me. I'm pretty sure no one in that theater has but a secondhand idea how *Bambi* ends because watching the dumb girl with the brown braids wrestle with a wrought iron balcony was a much more riveting show.

But I sure enough got to see what those boys were up to, and that made it fine that my ears were pink and raw for a week. You'd think curiosity of that magnitude, so powerful that it overrode common sense and maybe even the survival instinct, would have bred itself out of the gene pool by now, but I was evidence that it hadn't. I was on my way to the Big Chief Motor Lodge smelling like sandalwood, wearing clean clothes, and maybe, just maybe, I'd applied a light coat of mascara and honey-flavored lip gloss.

I hadn't yet explored the new motel. My home-away-from-home in cases of extreme mosquito invasions at the house was the Battle Lake Motel, a cute and clean log-cabin-sided destination across the street from the Big Chief. It wasn't directly on the banks of the lake, but it was friendly, family-owned, and hospitable. The Big Chief, on the other hand, was going for the sprawling resort look with its bland exterior and massive parking lot.

I pulled into the crammed parking lot of the two-story motel, staying in my car for ten minutes, studying the cream-colored building. I could hear the oompa-whomp of polka music emanating from the football field at the other edge of town. Not With My Horse didn't sound too bad from this distance. To my right was West Battle Lake and to my left was Highway 210. And in front of me was certainly my demise.

Like most motels, this one had exterior entrances for all the rooms. I counted six doors on top and four on the bottom, the bottom ones spread on each side of the brightly lit lobby. I assumed there was the same arrangement of rooms on the other side, the side facing the lake. Why, if this was about sex, would Johnny bring me here? He lived with his mom, whom he was taking care of after his dad had passed suddenly, and so there wasn't much privacy at his place, but why not come to mine?

Only one way to find out.

I sighed, left the safety of my car, and dragged my feet toward the lobby. I could see the full moon sparkling off the lake through the other side. The glass-sided lobby was a smart design choice. It made the place seem modern and steeped in nature at the same time. Room number 2 was immediately to the left of the main entrance and room number 3 was directly to the right. Above me, on the second floor, the rooms started at 5 and went to 10. It was a good bet room 20 was on the other side top floor, far right when facing the motel. I could walk through the lobby like I knew what I was doing, up the stairs, and knock confidently on the door. Or I could pee my pants and whistle Dixie. I decided on a compromise and went to the front desk, feeling like the Whore of Babylon.

I waited my turn. The combination of the Octoberfest weekend and the political candidates and their entourages in town for the debate seemed to have filled the motel to its rafters. In fact, I recognized the emcee from this morning, Sarah Glokkmann's redheaded assistant, Grace, in the front of the line. There appeared to be a mix-up in her room key because she was trading one plastic card for another. Seven minutes later, I was at the head of the line, still not sure what I was going to say.

"Um, I have a … well, I'm meeting someone in room 20 tonight, and I'm wondering if he, I mean, if *they* have checked in yet."

Donning her best gynecologist's face, the older woman behind the counter pressed a couple keys on her computer. I didn't recognize her, which hopefully meant she also didn't recognize me. "Ah yes, the Jacuzzi suite. Nicest room in the resort." She smiled at me, and my cheeks blazed red. "There's a fireplace in there, though it's maybe too warm tonight. Let's see. Yes. The other party checked in an hour ago."

"Thanks," I croaked. A Jacuzzi suite? What the hell? Mrs. Berns must have lied to me about Johnny's intentions, or she was blind to them herself. I lurched toward the lakeside door, my embarrassment turning to suspicion evolving to anger. Send me a fancy linen invitation booty call, my ass. It wouldn't be the first time I'd been fooled into believing some guy was a gentleman, and I knew exactly how to deal with this. I marched up the stairs, steaming past a vaguely familiar dark-haired man, down the cement walkway, and knocked loudly on the last door, number 20.

The answer was immediate. "I wasn't sure you'd come." Johnny stood on the other side of the door sporting a tuxedo that hugged his broad shoulders like a lover. His beautiful hair was curling thickly around his collar, and he pushed it back impatiently and stepped to the side, making room for me to enter. When he moved, I saw that he'd lit the fireplace, along with hundreds of candles. The Jacuzzi, thankfully, was not bubbling.

"How dare you," I said.

The look of embarrassed expectancy slipped off his face, replaced by confusion. "What?"

"You think just because you reserve a room and buy some candles that I'll sleep with you?"

He flinched as if I'd slapped him. "Mira, that's not it. I just wanted a quiet night with you, on neutral ground. To talk."

"Talk?" I jabbed a finger toward the candles behind him.

He dropped his gaze and ran his fingers through his hair. "I should know better than to listen to Mrs. Berns," he said under his breath. He brought his eyes back to mine, and like always, looking into those deep blues made my heart skip a beat. "Look, Mira. I didn't do this so you'd sleep with me. I'd love that, yeah, but that's not what tonight is about. Just give me a chance. One evening, fully-clothed, to convince you that I'm the right guy."

The angry, Tourette's-dusted mice in my brain were whizzing and scratching, goading me to say something mean or inappropriately funny to push Johnny away, again and for good. Before they could get the better of me, I threw myself into the room and bulldozed Johnny out of the way so I could slam the door shut. My mood swing gave me whiplash. "Okay. I'm in. But don't expect anything." Damn. One mouse must have escaped.

His grin broke open. He spread out his arms so I could take in the whole room. I couldn't resist the impish smile on his face. I turned to follow his gaze and saw a candlelit table with a white tablecloth. On top rested a gorgeous blooming African violet alongside a frosted bottle of sparkling grape juice and two champagne glasses, a pizza from Zorbaz—cheese and green olive, if my nose was not mistaken—

and enough Nut Goodie bars to kill a diabetic. Could he hear my heart breaking? Not wanting him to see the happiness on my face, I scurried toward the table.

"This is nice," I murmured, wondering how many slices of pizza I could eat without crossing a line.

He strolled past me, and I felt the heat of his body skimming my back as he moved to pull out a chair. "Madam." He indicated the seat and smiled boyishly. My lips couldn't resist. They smiled back before welcoming a boatload of pizza and chocolate.

I'd like to say I grew closer to Johnny that night, but it turns out I already knew him pretty well. Over the course of the meal, he filled me in on how his mom was doing and asked me about mine, told me about his plan for returning to the University of Madison next fall to begin his PhD in Horticulture, and gently probed me for more information about my past. His voice soothed the angry mice, and it wasn't long until I'd forgotten my misgivings about the night.

As our conversation fell into an easy give and take, I found myself desiring more than words. Without warning, my six-month dry spell had snuck up on my cowardice, slapped a chloroform rag over its mouth, and stuffed it in the closet. I became fixated on Johnny's lips, those strong cupid's bows, and I imagined what they would feel like on my neck, my lower back, my breasts.

Suddenly, I noticed that his mouth had stopped moving. "What?" I shot my gaze guiltily upward.

He smiled. "I said, are you okay? You've been quiet the last couple minutes. Do I have something on my teeth?"

I blushed and wiped the drool off my chin. "I'm fine." There's something really hot about a guy who respects you enough to provide your favorite meal and then backs off and waits for you to come to him. Problem was, I didn't know how to do that sober. A couple drinks in me and I'd be on him like white on rice, but without alcohol, I wasn't sure of the protocol.

I began by trying to shoot him mind rays suggesting he kiss me. After a few minutes, it became apparent that wasn't the most efficient method. And I flirted about as well as a pig wore shoes, so that only left the direct route. Get to your feet and kiss the man. Just do it. Take your future into your own hands, I told myself, and choose something good for once. I slammed back the last of my sparkling grape juice and stood, all glorious woman going after her man.

I tried, I really did, but halfway out of my seat, my nerves took over and forced me back down with an oof. I tossed some sort of half-hearted wink in the middle to try and distract from the failed attempt. Probably I looked like a twitchy ventriloquist's dummy, or a party balloon that someone gave up on. My dorkiness made me sick to my stomach, and I became acutely aware of the heat of the fireplace smelling like a hundred lighter flames and the candles reflecting my embarrassment back to me.

Johnny eyed me quizzically. "You sure you're okay, Mira? You look a little green."

I was feeling a little green. Who corrects themselves in mid-move? The only thing more embarrassing would have been to fall on him, or to snart midstep. Why not try all three? It'd be a trifecta of humiliation. Why was my heart racing? And since when had Johnny been standing over me? I thought he was across the table. How'd he reached me so quickly? Was he making the move? Were my lips glossy? I made a seductive prepucker. I could still pull this off. I could redeem myself. But gawd was it hot in here.

"I think you need to go to the bathroom."

"Huh?" If there was a list of things you *don't* want to hear when you think the man of your dreams is about to kiss you, that would be at the top. Before I could protest, he was leading me toward the bathroom. I caught a glimpse of myself in the wall mirror and was dismayed to see I was the color of St. Patrick's Day beer. Urp. That was it. The thought of beer pushed me over the edge. I leaned over the toilet, expelling a torrent of purple grape juice, red pizza, and brown chocolate.

"Don't worry, it's probably just a stomach bug," Johnny said, holding my hair back. "When I brought my mom in for her checkup, the doctor said it was going around."

The sweetness in his voice mortified me. I reached for the toilet handle to erase the evidence, but it was immediately replaced by more. Twenty minutes of heaving later, I was spent, having only the energy to calculate how long it would take to obtain a passport so I could fly to India to officially pursue my future as an untouchable. Johnny handed me a warm, wet towel, and I cleaned off my face. He left the bathroom, closing the door to give me some privacy, and returned a few minutes later, knocking softly before handing me a toothbrush and miniature toothpaste from the front desk. I accepted both gratefully.

"I'm so sorry," I said, after I was as cleaned up as a person could be after involuntarily expelling olives through her nose. My throat felt like a sand truck had driven through it. I couldn't look at him. "Is this your worst date ever?"

He smiled, his eyes twinkling. "No, my worst date ever was the first night at the State Fair when you ran away before I could kiss you."

I thrust out my hand in horror.

"Don't worry," he said. "I'm not going to try and kiss you now. Just come over to the bed and lie down. You'll feel better in the morning."

"I want to go home," I moaned, trying to stand. A wave of dizziness pushed me back onto the closed toilet seat. "Or, maybe I'll just lie down for a little while."

"Good idea," he said, hoisting me into his arms and carrying me to the soft bed. "Tiger Pop and Luna can get out if they want to?"

I nodded, sinking into the mattress.

"OK. I have to leave for work at 5:00 a.m. I'll head out early to check on them first, okay? Just sleep." He felt my forehead and then covered me with a spare blanket before stretching out behind me, one arm draped loosely across my waist, reminding me I wasn't alone.

And that's all I remembered until I heard the scream.

FIVE

MY DISORIENTATION WAS TOTAL. The room was black. It didn't smell familiar, and the digital clock was in the wrong place telling me some crap about 5:34. Where was I, and why had I been dreaming of moving to West Bengal? That's when it came back to me in smelly waves of shame. Argh. I was pretty sure Johnny had seen me hurl last night. The humiliation was smothering.

And then it pierced my ears again, a scream as chilling as morgue water, the noise that had woken me. I sprung out of bed and was shoved back by a Mack truck of a headache. I powered through and felt my way to the door, focusing on a sliver of grayish light glowing through the curtains. I found the doorknob and turned it, welcoming the fresh and chilly lake air. West Battle's waves were choppy and dark, the sun an hour and a half from rising. The only brightness issued from a lonely light in the parking lot. People were beginning to stir about in their rooms, but as of yet only two doors were open, mine and the one immediately to my right. A cleaning cart was resting between our rooms. I skirted it and entered the adjacent room gingerly, certain the scream had emanated from there.

I was paralyzed by what I saw.

In the middle of the room lay a crumpled male figure. A cleaning woman knelt next to the man, searching for a pulse. It was then that I noticed the jellied outline of a clear plastic bag over his head and the preternatural stillness that only death can bring.

I raced to the bedside phone to dial 911.

"Already called," the cleaning lady said. "Besides, there's no hurry."

Her calmness unsettled me. "Were you the one who just screamed?"

"Yeah," she said, leaning back on her heels. "This room was supposed to be empty. I was startled, is all. But you clean hotel rooms for enough years, and nothing really scares you anymore." She indicated the plastic bag. "Must have suffocated himself. It's tight around his neck."

I didn't want to get too close, didn't want to see whose face it was, but I found myself tiptoeing around the body at a safe distance, just the same. And that's how I came to stare into the dead eyes of Bob Webber, the blogger who would never again care if the world spelled his name with one or two b's.

SIX

"SHIT. I OWE CURTIS ten bucks."

The familiar voice at the door yanked me sharply from the frozen horror on Mr. Webber's chalk-white face. One edge of his forehead appeared darker than the rest and soft, like he'd hit the ground hard. He was still dressed in his sad, shabby coat. "Mrs. Berns?" I asked. She looked tiny in the doorway, tiny and crazy-sexy in thigh-high stockings and a black teddy under a translucent, feather-lined robe. "What are you doing here?"

She took in my bedhead and bloodshot eyes courtesy of an evening of power hurling. "We'll have the talk when you get a little bit older, honey. We have a more important situation on our hands. You just cost me ten cucumbers."

Bernard, the stuffy reporter who yesterday had been in her room at the Senior Sunset, materialized behind her, looking ridiculously bird-legged in boxer shorts and a white v-neck T-shirt.

"Wah?" I asked.

She crossed her arms and leaned into the door frame. "We have a Mira and Corpse pool at the Senior Sunset. Curtis Poling bet you couldn't make it through Octoberfest weekend without finding a dead body. I figured if I steered you away from your usual haunts and kept a close eye on you, I'd win the bet. Turns out you can't trick luck as bad as yours, sweetie pie."

"Wait, is that why you talked Johnny into bringing me here? To win a ten-dollar bet?" Nothing like indignation to arrest your attention.

"Pah." She strode over to the corpse and knelt down to stare at his face. "It's that Leeson boy we should feel sorry for. How'd you humiliate yourself this time? And who's the wormfood here?"

"Bob Webber," Bernard said from behind us.

"One b or two?" I asked, staring at the face of the deceased and wondering why he looked so frightened. My experience with corpses is that most of them left the world with a disgusted looked on their faces, a final "Really? Is that all?" Bob Webber, on the other hand, looked like his last moments had been awfully scary.

"Two."

"Well now, how do you know him?" Mrs. Berns asked, turning toward her date and sounding peeved.

Bernard cleared his throat. "He operated *The Body Politic* blog. Well-known in the business of political reporting, a reputation for mendacity."

I didn't like the guy's arrogance, and I didn't trust his aim with big words. "Mendacity or tenacity?"

"My dear girl, he didn't give up when he had a story. He was efficacious." He talked slowly to give me the opportunity to dig out my thinking cap.

I pointed at the plastic bag sealed tightly around the corpse's neck. "Was he going through tough times?"

"I didn't know him personally," Bernard answered.

I stared from Bernard to Mrs. Berns and back again. "Where did you two meet?"

"Gas station." Mrs. Berns stood and grabbed Bernard's hand. "Time to go, honey." She shot her most threatening look to the cleaning lady, which was difficult to pull off in her Victoria's Oldest Secret regalia. "We were never here."

The maid rolled her eyes and reached into her apron for a squirt of Purel, leaving me to decide if I also should never have been here. Lots of questions get asked when you're standing near a dead body, suicide or no. Besides, my eyes and throat were scratchy and my stomach was still unsettled. I backed out of the room, pausing long enough outside to lift the room list from the maid's cart and slide it into my jeans pocket before returning to room 20 to retrieve my car keys and purse.

My plan was to scurry down the walkway and never look back, but once past the cart I was slowed by an agitated-looking Grace, barreling toward me. I stepped aside to let her enter room 18, her hands shaking as she slid in the electronic key card. She didn't make eye contact with me, acted, in fact, as if she dearly hoped she were invisible. When the door glided closed behind her, I had enough time to note that both the beds were made. I returned to room 19 for a moment, peeping my head in. The maid was dragging on an Eve's Slim in the entirely smoke-free motel, studying the body in the center as if she were considering whether to get one for her den.

"Did you clean room 18 yet?"

She shook her head in the negative. "This is my first room of the day. It was supposed to be empty," she repeated.

I thanked her and made my way to my car just as a wailing ambulance pulled into the lot, followed by a navy blue Battle Lake police cruiser with its cherries on. What I spied in the police car froze me until a basic instinct kicked in. I zipped to my left and launched between two four-door sedans. I skinned my knees in the process but it would be completely worth it if I was right and that was Gary Wohnt, former chief of the Battle Lake Police Department, persona non grata since August, behind the wheel of the cop car.

"You okay?"

I looked into the clear brown eyes of a man in his late fifties. He was sitting cross-legged in the space between the two cars I was now occupying. His clothes were worn but serviceable, and if not for the smell of BO and his odd location, he looked like Everyman. "Why're you sitting between two cars in a parking lot?"

"Why're you?"

He had a point. I shot a glance over my shoulder to see if the cop car was parking nearby. "I tripped."

"Pretty spectacular trip," he said, rubbing his chin. "Not that you asked, but when I need to hide from the police, I find it most effective to *not* draw attention to myself. For example, I don't start my hair on fire, yell 'help,' or leap into the air and land between two cars like a handicapped gazelle."

"Point taken." I looked away from the emergency vehicles to study him for a moment. "Hey, were you one of the protestors at the debate yesterday?"

"I am." He held out his hand. "Randy Martineau. Pleased to meet you."

I shook it. "You get a chance to talk to Swydecker and Glokkmann at the debate?"

"Swydecker, yes. Glokkmann, no. She executed her usual escape."

"You at the motel to corner her?"

"Something like that." He nodded toward the far end of the parking lot. The Battle Lake police car and ambulance pulled around to the other side, out of sight. "I think you're in the clear."

I relaxed marginally and tried to push my hair out of my eyes, but it moved as a mass, more post-hurling-restless-sleep-dreadlock than tress. "Thank you. Now if you'll excuse me, I have to shower, brush my teeth with a sander, and get to work."

He nodded, seeming to give my list serious consideration. "If you duck behind that yellow VW and then scurry toward the Hummer, there's a line of bushes that should get you all the way to the back of the parking lot."

"Thanks," I said. It wasn't until I was safely behind the wheel of my car and out of town that I wondered how he knew where I'd parked. That concern sparked a realization: the vaguely familiar man I had passed on the stairwell last night on my way to the Night of Humiliation with Johnny had been Bob Webber. He hadn't been carrying any bags, and if I replayed the brief encounter in my head, I remembered him appearing agitated, though I'd been too deep in my own problems to make more than passing note of it.

I pulled the room list I had pinched from my pocket and scanned it while driving. It consisted of three columns: the first with room numbers, the second with last names, and the third with duration of stay. Glokkmann and Swydecker snagged my attention first. They were both staying on the same level as I had and were checking out today. I found Webber, but his room had been on the other side of the hotel, right next to the lobby door: room 4. And he was supposed to have checked out yesterday morning. What room had I seen him come from last night? And more pressing, what in the hell was Gary Wohnt doing back in town?

SEVEN

TRUE TO HIS WORD, Johnny had stopped by the doublewide to fetch Luna and Tiger Pop fresh food and water. Tiger Pop looked particularly haughty, and so I guessed Johnny must have given her some good ear-scratching, too. The African violet that had been the centerpiece at our table last night was on the counter top, blooming purpily next to a brief note:

I hope you feel better today! We'll talk soon.

Not if I could help it. I didn't need a psychic to tell me this relationship was cursed. Nope. It was back to all Chief Wenonga, all the time for this woman. The decision made my heart heavy, but it was for the best, for Johnny and me.

My hot shower felt heavenly, and I brushed my teeth for two full minutes, managing to wonder only briefly what had driven me to lift the guest list from the cleaner's cart. I didn't know Bob, and no one but Johnny, Mrs. Berns, and Bernard knew that I had spent the night at the motel. Nope, look forward instead of back. That was my new motto. I crumpled the list into a ball and tossed it into the nearest basket and reached for clean clothes.

I still had a light headache and my stomach was not interested in entertaining company, but I had a day of work to stumble through. The library didn't open until noon on Sundays, but I had to snap photos of dancers at the a.m. Bavaria Boogie-thon for the paper, the last of my Octoberfest newspaper assignments, before heading to the library early to type up the Glokkmann/Swydecker debate article. Then, a short, five-hour shift and back to my blessed bed. I stepped into my room to look at it, warm sunlight falling on my fluffy duvet, and almost wept. "Soon," I whispered. "I'll be back soon."

As consolation, I made time to tend to my indoor plants. To say I love to garden is like saying I don't mind being sane. Having my fingers in dirt and smelling the peppery spice of fresh-crushed leaves grounds me and keeps me from walking naked through town wearing only a pair of mukluks, asking for purple space cookies and hugs, or any other various shades of crazy I'd adopt if it weren't for my connection to the soil.

Living in Minnesota, creativity was a requirement if I was to stay on my rocker in the colder months, and this year I was prepared. I'd ordered two dwarf orange and lemon trees from a catalog along with a spice house, a miniature indoor greenhouse that hung from the ceiling by a plant hook in direct sunlight. The front of Sunny's doublewide was a huge bay window facing the lake in which my succulents, ferns, ivies, and now tropical fruits and spices vied for golden rays. The orange and lemon trees had a rough start but were presently bursting with sweet-scented white blossoms. The orange tree even had a pea-sized, rebelliously lime-green fruit hard as a nugget nestled in a bundle of leaves. I gently patted the baby fruit each time I watered it.

The spices were at the gawky toddler stage, clumsy heads bending their slim stalks. They'd just started to distinguish themselves from one another, the parsley bursting ridges along the previously-smooth edges of its leaves to set itself apart from the basil still primly holding to its spade-shape. I also had cilantro, oregano, spiky thyme, and a dill I'd planted for comic relief. Every time I parted the plastic to water the seedlings, I was enveloped in the warm, brown and green scent of growing things, and it made my heart jump. I was in love with plants. Give me Chief Wenonga and a garden, and I'd call life good.

I stepped outside into the appropriately gray day and turned back to grab a scarf. It was cold. The change of seasons was upon us. My car windows even sported a light layer of rime, but not enough to require a scraper beyond the side of my hand. I drove in on the west side of town to avoid passing the motel. This route took me past the Trinity Lutheran Church, which was more packed than usual. As I cruised past, I counted at least a dozen camera crews outside. At the debate yesterday, both candidates had promised that they'd be attending church this morning, Glokkmann at the Catholic church and Swydecker at the Lutheran, but that didn't seem particularly newsworthy. Shows what I know about politics.

Parking in the high school parking lot for the second time in as many days, I was struck at how trampled the grounds looked compared to yesterday. Glittering beer bottles littered the frost-crunched grass. I grabbed the digital camera and strode toward the main tent, the sour smell of a day-old party assaulting my nostrils and sliding down the back of my throat like thick oil. My stomach bucked, but I persevered. For all my laziness, I had a good work ethic, and snapping photos was a job I enjoyed. At least I used to enjoy it. Unfortunately, what was sashaying out of the main tent and toward me wearing clothes like a truck wore tires could squeeze the joy out of potato chips.

"Honey, is that the new Goth look you're sporting? It doesn't sit so well on you. With those high cheekbones and deep-set eyes, you look like Skeletor." She walked up to air kiss me, enveloping me in a cloud of oily perfume. "Never mind that. I was hoping to run into you today. Have I got a business proposition for you!"

I coughed, idly wondering if I had been Pol Pot in a past lifetime. This much bad luck did not spring forth organically. I disregarded her proposition and studied her. Usually, with Kennie Rogers, current mayor and self-appointed police chief of the Battle Lake Police Department, it's the clothes that attract your eyes. This time, it was the color of her skin. "Why are you orange?"

She pushed her lips together. "I am not orange. I'm Bahama Brown."

I shrugged. One woman's Bahama Brown is another woman's Tangerine Terror. "If you'll excuse me, I've got work to do."

Kennie and I had an odd relationship. Actually, Kennie had an odd relationship with the world. She'd spent her whole life in Battle Lake, carving out a niche for herself on the local political scene, all bluster and bossiness. Last May, I'd uncovered a tragic chapter in her beauty queen past. She'd overcome that and still clung to her youthful beauty with claws and a mascara wand, dressed like a teenage girl with a time machine, occasionally adopted a Southern accent, and was cannier than Chef Boyardee. She was only ten years older than me and had earned my grudging respect, though I'd sooner switch wardrobes with her than let her know. Ultimately, I avoided her when I could because she was always more trouble than she was worth.

"Yes you do! You're my test dummy."

She was probably half right. "I'm *not* your test dummy."

She grabbed my hand and shook it. "Okay, then you're the new Vice President of the Kennie Rogers Corporation, LLC."

"Pass."

"You don't want to make $250 in one hour?"

Kennie was notorious for her business schemes, the most recent ones involving nudity, coffins, and sheep. "I really don't."

She talked over me, and not for the first time. In an effort to distract myself from her words, I forced myself to truly acknowledge her outfit. It was a catsuit sewn of some shiny red and blue fabric, and this cat had caught more than her share of mice. Odd puffs of flesh bulged over and under the gold belt ringing her waist, and across her chest was a huge yellow "S." She looked chilly enough to cut diamonds with her chest. I shouldn't have been surprised that she was wearing shiny-white running shoes. In the tent behind us, the wheeze-oom-pah-whomp-whomp of accordion music was starting right on time.

"Sure. That's nice," I said, when she paused. I hadn't heard a word.

"Wonderful. Tuesday night. Bronze and Bond Speed Dating begins!"

"Hunh?"

"It'll be fantabulous. I've reserved the party room at Stub's. We'll have privacy booths set up, and you're in charge of spray tanning anyone with a coupon. Come a little early so you can help me decorate the dating tables. After we've tanned our clients into a sexy version of themselves, everyone goes to their assigned dating seat. Each person gets three minutes before moving to the next table in search of the love of their life. Maybe we should come up with conversation cards? Fun!"

Fun like cramps. "I'm not going to spray strangers with orange body paint."

She hummed. "Already said you would..."

I felt like I was falling, and leapt for practicality. "Everyone in this town already knows each other. Why would they sign up for speed dating?"

"Haven't you been listening? There's been another murder! That always brings fresh blood to town."

EIGHT

"Back it up. What?"

"This morning. A dead man found at the new motel."

I didn't want to give away my recent proximity to the corpse so played it cool. "That's horrible! But how do you know it wasn't suicide?"

She eyed me suspiciously for a second, but was distracted when the tent flap opened and a strapping farmboy in tights and short-pants, a feathered cap perched on his head, stepped out to calm his pre-polka nerves with a cigarette. "Unlikely," she said, reapplying her lip gloss. "The body was found in a second-floor room, bag over his head to make it look like suicide, but he wasn't blue. The coroner said the lips of a person who dies of suffocation are always blue. And probably their fingernails. But this guy was as white as a sheet. His best guess is that someone killed the man by smashing his head in and then bagged it like a cantaloupe."

A chill crept out from my stomach and trickled down to my fingers and toes. Studying the death scene in my mind's eye, I knew she was right. Bob Webber, whiter than cream, the skin on the side of his forehead soft-looking, like a rug draped over a hole. I tried to play back other details to see if I'd missed anything, but I'd been too blurry-eyed from a lousy night's sleep and too certain it was a suicide to scope out the room. "Suspects?" I asked.

"Too early to know for sure, but everyone who was in the motel is being questioned."

Her words induced an ice bath that made my skin dimple. Had Johnny put my name on the room? "Probably a lot of out-of-towners staying there for the festival."

"Probably. Swydecker and Glokkmann were there for sure." She said Glokkmann's name with a perverse sneer, and I wondered if the two of them had a past. They must be close in age, I judged, and had grown up in the same neck of the woods. "But so far we know that Glokkmann and at least one of her people don't have an alibi for last night."

I let out a deep breath. Better Glokkmann than me. "Shouldn't you be there right now, being as you're the Chief of Police?"

She clapped her hands and her face lit up. "I left as soon as I realized what a tremendous business opportunity this would be. The tanning/speed dating idea initially started percolating when I got my first spray tan last night in Elbie Johanssen's basement. I thought, why couldn't I do this? Then, when I heard the murder announced over the police scanner this morning, I thought, new people in town! And who doesn't want to be romanced when they're feeling all tan and sexy? The plan came together like peanut butter and jelly. I pulled on this outfit and headed directly to the motel."

That meant she hadn't bought the speedy catsuit specifically for her business. It had already been hanging in her closet. I found myself wondering what the heck she had on deck. "And you managed to get your picture taken in your speedsuit by many swarming reporters?"

"If we're lucky."

"Aren't you concerned about finding the killer?"

She returned her full attentions to me, her eyes glittering, mouth in a sharp smile. "I'll leave that up to our new police deputy, a Mr. Gary Wohnt."

With the mention of his name, my skinned knees began smarting. "Wohnt *is* back." It didn't come out as a question.

Gary had been Kennie's biggest fan and rumored lover when I'd first met him, following her everywhere like a solemn puppy dog. That all changed when he met another woman in August and skipped town with the deeply religious hussy. I was willing to bet there was a story there, and I didn't want to hear it. I just wanted to stay as far from Wohnt as possible. He'd been the lead man on more than one of the murder investigations I'd had the ill fortune to get tangled up in. To say he and I weren't friends would be like saying that oil didn't mind vinegar so much. And he really was back in town, although apparently demoted.

My head was full.

"You don't look so good. Worse than usual, I mean. You need an aspirin or something?"

I hung my head in my hands. "I need to take some pictures, get through my library shift, and then marry my bed."

Kennie clucked. "Whatever. Say, a little Bahama Brown would brighten you right up. I've got the sprayer in my car. Sure you don't want a couple spritzes?"

"I'm sure."

"Don't say I didn't offer. I'll see you Tuesday night. Ta ta!"

She swirled off, leaving me to contemplate the big picture. Here were the facts: short of simultaneously walking into a wall and pooping my pants, there was not much left in my Johnny Leeson humiliation repository. I had stumbled across a murdered body this morning, but only three people knew that, and of that three, the only two who knew my name were equally as invested in not being identified with the crime scene. Although it was certainly tragic the blogger had been murdered, it was none of my business. Gary Wohnt was back, and he excelled at making me miserable, which was another whole reason for remaining uninvested in the murder investigation. I added up the facts again and came to the same blessed conclusion: avoid Johnny and Gary, and life was golden.

Life in order, I held my nose and stepped into the tent to snap photos of knock-kneed men twirling women in tulle. The music under the big top was so loud it knocked out any other thoughts, leaving only a low-level repulsion as the odors of sauerkraut and sweat mingled on the dance floor.

The goal of the Bavarian Boogie-thon was to be the last dancer standing, no breaks given. However, not wanting to cut into tonight's continuation of drinking and dancing for all, the sponsors of the dance-off had wisely added spoilers. The first was a release of piglets onto the stage, which couldn't have sounded good even on paper. When that didn't stop anyone from boogying, a quick break was called to strap ankle-weights to the contestants. That picked off the outliers, leaving six core couples who appeared prepared to polka their way through the Apocalypse. I cut out just as another intermission was announced to tie one leg of each couple together, followed by a mandatory round of Jägermeister shots. I left confident that today's event would be the briefest dance-off in history.

I slid into my car and drove to the mercifully empty library lot, cruising inside to e-mail Ron the photos and peck out a story:

Battle Lake Hosts Political Debate

On Saturday, October 17, Battle Lake played host to the major party representative candidates for Congressional District 7. Current Representative Sarah Glokkmann, a native of Henning, and Arnold Swydecker, former Superintendent of the Detroit Lakes school district, met to discuss their goals for our district's political future.

"I support our country and our troops," Representative Glokkmann emphasized, while Mr. Swydecker believed that, "we have to make some hard choices now to prepare for the future."

Both candidates spoke briefly before responding to questions e-mailed to the City of Battle Lake by Minnesota voters. They ended by answering questions from those in attendance. Representative Glokkmann refused to commit to a future run for Minnesota's Governor seat.

Glokkmann and Swydecker helped to kick off Battle Lake's 27th annual Octoberfest. This was their final debate of the campaign season. Both will be stumping individually between now and the November 2nd election.

While I was online, I briefly researched both candidates. The first hits were their websites, which were cluttered and boring. The next page or two of links connected to newspaper articles, the majority of them better written than mine but still not interesting. Next I checked out *The Body Politic*, which was easy to locate. I hated to admit it, but the exposés were fascinating. Webber had been a genuine investigative reporter, and the stories I skimmed showed someone dedicated to deep research.

He also had a pit bull's focus on Sarah Glokkmann. At least 30 percent of the headline articles delved into her political misdealing. If she really intended to run for governor in two years, she had some messes to clean up, if Bob was right. I wondered why none of the muck he had uncovered—vote-buying bribes from the oil industry, using state funds to take her kids on shopping trips to New York City, missing key votes in the House due to a drinking problem—was in the mainstream newspaper articles. Maybe he'd made it all up. Maybe it didn't matter to me.

Working at the computer was reigniting my headache and I shut it down at 11:30. Still not hungry, I decided to open the front door early, stepping outside to suck in some fresh air before the official work began. On my way back in, I grabbed the six paperbacks out of the Returned Books bin. Three mysteries, two sci fi, and a nonfiction book about the power of positive thinking. I set that one on the edge of the trash can to see if it could get itself out of a jam.

I limped to the back room to see what I had for headache relief and found a bottle of generic ibuprofen that had only expired three years ago. I chewed a handful, downed it with mud-flavored tap water, and returned to the main room of the library, where I sank gratefully into a bean bag chair in the children's section. If I could only stay here forever, I thought as I petted Nut Goodie, the stuffed ferret I'd been trying to give away for two months. I rested Nut on my belly and closed my eyes for a moment, imagining a magic world full of bean bags, rainbows, and not one single corpse.

———

It wasn't a sound so much as an itchy feeling that woke me, a silly grin still on my face. I'd been dreaming of butterflies and popcorn and it must have induced a smile just big enough to let escape a sizeable pool of drool. That was the second sensation I experienced after the itchy danger one—wetness. I lifted my head to spy what had awakened me and ran the back of my hand across my moist cheek. I must have been out cold because my eyes didn't open at the same time, one a few beats sleepier than the other.

And so it was that my left eye had the good sense to be scared before my right eye even heard there was a party.

NINE

You'd think most men would look alike from the knees on down, I thought as I studied Gary Wohnt's shiny black shoes and polyester pants from my bean bag roost. I was careful not to move my open eye or unhinge my second, my on-the-fly theory being that if I played it cool, he might think I was simply having a seizure and leave me alone. But dang if that open eye wasn't getting dry. I always lost the staring contests growing up. If only I'd known how handy that skill would be in later life, I might have tried harder.

I blinked and sighed deeply. I didn't possess the energy to launch a full-on offensive but mustered what I could. "Well, well, well, look who's back. Miss us?" I tried standing archly but stumbled at the blood rush. Gary caught me and pushed me against the wall with one strong arm, pinning me like a bug.

He was an olive-skinned man with dark eyes that he liked to hide behind cop sunglasses, the kind that reflected all your shortcomings right back at you. I'd had to stifle many a spontaneous confession because of those glasses. And he didn't court small talk. "Where were you last night?"

"Hmm, did we have a date? I don't remember."

He kept staring. Or doing blinky eye-strengthening exercises. It was impossible to tell on this side of the glasses.

I continued. "In fact, last I heard, you were totally off the market, gallivanting around the country with a, what was she, gospel singer?"

His mouth set in a line that made clear he'd never gallivanted a day in his life and that I best shut my piehole, but anxiety kept me talking well past the point of good sense. "Or a candy striper? Hard to remember. Hey, have you had a chance to talk to Kennie since you got back? You two used to date, didn't you?"

He took his arm away, and I slumped a little but kept standing. The sparkles I'd seen upon shooting up too quickly slowly receded. And I still hadn't answered his question. "So why do you want to know where I was last night?"

For a moment, I didn't think he was going to respond, but he finally said, "Just routine questioning related to an investigation."

"What's the investigation about?" I noticed the badge on this uniform was smaller than his police chief badge, but his gun looked just as big.

"A possible murder."

"I didn't kill anybody." I turned off my sassy box quick-like and attempted a relaxed, "How ridiculous would that be?" smile. It felt jack-o-lanternish. That's when I realized I'd arranged my questions in the wrong order. "Who was killed?"

"Why don't you tell me where you were last night, and I can continue the investigation."

The only autonomic function I could rely on, apparently, was my liar. "I spent the night with Mrs. Berns." Only a half-lie, really.

The corner of his mouth twitched, either a smile being born and killed or frustration seeking an outlet. "Really. Where?"

"Not in the same bed, if that's what you're asking." For the love of Pete, had my brain gone on a cruise, leaving my mouth to fend for herself? She didn't do so well alone.

"At the Big Chief Motor Lodge?"

It took all my willpower not to blanch. "I've heard that place is really nice. Is it open already?"

"Because a source tells me that four people were on the scene before police arrived: a motel employee, an elderly woman wearing Frederick's of Hollywood gear, her boy candy, and a brunette in her 30s who, I quote, 'looked like she'd been rode hard and put away wet.'" That twitch again at his lips.

I swelled up, indignant and about to protest before I realized I probably still looked that way. "I've got a house right outside of town, Ch-... Deputy Wohnt. Why in the world would I want to stay in a hotel?" Had he always been so muscular? I thought I remembered him as a little rounder in the belly.

I saw an eyebrow appear briefly above the mirrored glass. "I wondered the same thing."

I pursed my lips and shook my head in agreement so it looked like I was on his wondering team. Finally, prudence had slapped a leash on my tongue.

The radio on his shoulder squawked a code, and he responded tersely. "On my way." He returned his attention to me. "We have more talking to do. Everyone who was at the motel last night has been asked not to leave town. I'd recommend, if you are one of them, that you also choose not to leave."

Where was I going to go? Besides to hell. In a hand basket. I gave him the thumbs up. "Is that all? 'Cuz I've got work to do." I didn't even know what time it was. Maybe I could go home.

"No, I'm afraid that isn't all." His demeanor shifted, and for the first time, I saw a hint of human in him. "Mrs. Berns got in a car accident late this morning. She's in the ICU at the Douglas County Hospital."

TEN

I WAS FOUR WHEN I entered my first hospital. My mom took me to visit a friend who'd had her appendix removed. It was exciting. People bustled down long hallways, fresh flowers were displayed everywhere, and a good percentage of the population got to lie around in their pajamas and watch TV. The antiseptic smell raised some prehistoric hackles, but that fear instinct was overridden when I spotted the free hot soup-hot tea-hot chocolate-hot coffee dispenser in the waiting room. Chicken noodle soup that came in a box was a treat reserved for when I was very sick, and here, in the middle of this busy room where no one would notice what a little girl did, was all the yellow broth I could walk away with.

Looking back, even in a pre-litigious society, the Hot Drink Caddy was a banana peel next to pit of razor blades. On one side, it meted out your powder of choice—the dehydrated chicken broth was the color of acid sunshine, the hot cocoa powder a purplish brown, the coffee a grainy mahogany shade, and the tea a black powder with murky bits of dried lemon peel. Anyone waiting for news of their loved one and in need of some soothing hot beverage had simply to pull the Lucite handle on the front of the appropriate powder and a chute would open delivering a sandy, slinking mound into the bottom of a paper cup, available in the Dixie cup dispenser attached to the machine.

Getting the powder was the easy part. The hangman's noose lay on the opposite side in the form of a modified hot water dispenser, the kind that you find on an industrial coffee machine, just a simple silver tap that delivered water roughly the temperature of the center of the earth. In retrospect, the mastermind who had invented the Hot Drink Caddy must have sensed some element of danger, some dearth of common sense vaguely tied to pairing paper cups with rushing volcanic liquid. That was the only explanation for why he had made the tap lower than average, about waist height for an adult male. Unfortunately, this put it at neck height for a four-year old girl unable to resist the unorthodox attraction of sipping rehydrated chicken broth from a paper cup between meals in a hospital.

In an era when seatbelts didn't retract on their own and child safety seats were for dollies, it wasn't hard to sneak away from your mom. Twist and skip, and there I was, white paper cup in hand, medicine-yellow powder sifting down the chute. I can still smell the acrid, sweaty chicken broth, all bright and rich, puffing as it hit the bottom of my cup with a soft sound, like a moth falling to earth. Cup in hand, mom busy at the information desk, I walked the Green Mile to the scalding water dispenser. I earned a friendly smile from a man waiting his turn, but that's the only acknowledgment I received before I stood on tiptoes to lift the red rectangle on the back of the silver spigot and let flow hissing, steaming, boiling water two inches behind my cup and onto my chest. I howled but didn't let go of the spigot, and the fiery water kept flowing. I don't know if it was the man behind me who yanked my hand away, or my mother after she flew over the heads of people seated in the waiting room to gather me in her arms without ever touching the ground between.

The next hour was a flurry. I remember tears, some mine, salve that smelled like banana Vaseline, and white bandages that I couldn't take off for ten days encircling me like a mummy. And that's forever what hospitals would be for me. Shitty places that looked like paradise until you tried to fill a paper cup with fake chicken broth, and then watch out. Burn, scream, and in you go.

"I'm here for Mrs. Berns. Can I see her?" I didn't want that desperation in my voice. If I wasn't scared, then there wouldn't be a reason to be scared. The hospital felt huge and cold. Nobody here would understand how much was at stake.

The woman smiled vaguely from behind her long, speckled laminate countertop, finishing what she was typing on her computer before glancing at me. She had an innocuous face, the Minnesota-bland countenance of a woman who dreamed of a world where people understood that she didn't gossip because she liked it, but rather because it was her duty to help others. "Are you family?"

"I'm her granddaughter," I lied. "I was told she was in a serious car accident, and I need to see her right away."

"Oh no," the woman said, returning her eyes to her computer. "That's no good. Let me see what I can find." She clicked for almost forty seconds, reading so slowly that I wanted to smack her on the side of the head with the pile of manila folders lying next to her and turn the screen toward me. Her expression changed before she looked back at me, a flash of I-don't-know-what skimming her face. "She's in room 256. Good luck."

I didn't bother with a response. I elbowed my way through the bustle of the main lobby and followed the arrows and the signs, taking a wrong turn at oncology before ending up on the edge of the ICU.

"Can I help you?"

I stopped before the swinging doors, startled by the woman behind the desk guarding the entrance. I realized I was breathing heavy. "I'm here to see Mrs. Berns. Room 256. I'm her granddaughter."

"You'll need to sign in."

"Fine." She handed me a clipboard with a lined sheet on it. I scribbled "Mira Berns" in blue ink on the line next to room 256, dropped the pen, and pushed my way through, counting the numbers on the wall outside of each room. Room 256 was across the hall from the ICU nurse's station. I wondered if that was good or bad. The door was framed with pumpkins cut from orange construction paper, black lines bisecting toothy grins and triangle eyes.

Her door was cracked. I stayed in the hall another moment, my head feeling white and cottony. The sterile, sick-sweet smell of surgery began to coat the lining of my nose. I pushed against her door, acutely aware of the pinkness of my hand against the brown wood. Inside, a curtain shielded the bed from my view. On my side of the curtain, a man and a woman, both near retirement age, were arguing heatedly. The man had salt-and-pepper hair tailored in a precise crew cut and slicked up with some sort of cream, the kind of pomade that would smell like your grandpa if you got too close. His nose was sharp enough to slice paper. The woman had the same nose but her hair was a chocolate brown, the deep lines around her eyes and nose declaring it a dye. I didn't recognize either of them, though I did know the director of the nursing home, who was standing off to the side, running his fingers through his hair and looking like he'd rather be at the proctologist.

All three of them glanced over when I walked in, but I didn't stop to ask questions because if I stopped, I would never be able to regain the momentum to look behind the curtain. I darted around the cloth divider, and my breathing stopped. There she lay, fragile and bandaged. Every visible centimeter of her was swathed in white, some of it leaking red, some tinged with a wet-looking brownish-yellow. The only perceptible movement was a catheter bag hung off to the side, dripping slowly full, its contents cloudy. The air around the bed smelled murky.

"Mira." The nursing home director took my arm and pulled me back. I couldn't remember his name. I'd interviewed him once or twice in my role as part-time reporter, but as a general rule, I avoided close contact with authority figures.

"Is she okay?" Stupid question. I don't know where it came from, who spoke it, even though my lips had moved.

"It's not …" He paused.

"What?"

"It's Freda Skolen."

The greedy wash of relief left me woozy. I knew Freda. She and her sister Ida shared a room at the Senior Sunset, and they were sweet, smart ladies. But they weren't my Mrs. Berns. "Where is she?"

"They took her to surgery over an hour ago. She's got a broken leg, three broken ribs, and a possible skull fracture. She's in tough shape, but it looks like she and Freda will pull through."

I'd had enough bad news in my life that I couldn't take his word for it. "I need to see her."

He shot a look at the other pair in the room and then back at me. "You're welcome to stay. The head nurse said Mrs. Berns would be out of recovery and back in her room by dinner. Actually, if you're willing to wait for her, I can get back. A lot of people in Battle Lake want to know how these two are doing."

"You're lucky they're alive," hissed the man, who'd stopped in his argument with the woman to watch me like a pickpocket. He slid his eyes off of me and onto the director, his knife-edged nose cutting the air.

His companion grabbed his arm. She wasn't much taller than my 5'6" but had the sturdy build of a Swedish farmwife. Her strong fingers held his arm firmly. "That's enough, Conrad. We can decide what to do once we find out how mom is."

Conrad Berns, Mrs. Berns' oldest son, the one who'd committed her to the home almost ten years earlier? I held out my hand, my mind racing. "I'm Mira James. A friend of Mrs. Berns. You're her son?"

The director chose that moment to duck out, giving my shoulder a grateful squeeze as he passed. Conrad watched him go but didn't stop him. "I've heard of you. You let my mother work for you at the library."

I bristled. "Mrs. Berns is an adult. She makes her own decisions. I don't 'let' her do anything." If only he knew how true that was.

"And you took her to the State Fair?"

Now didn't seem to be the time to argue that in fact she had hitch-hiked to the State Fair and appropriated the only bedroom in my loaner RV. I tried switching roles. "You live in Fargo?"

"Yes."

"Retired?

"Forty years in the Navy."

That explained the haircut. And now that you mention it, the military posture. Dang that he really did smell like my grandpa up close, though. It inclined me to warm up to him a hair, as much as I didn't want to. "How's Mrs., um, your mom doing?"

He seemed to sense that he'd regained the upper hand. "We'll see shortly. You're welcome to stay until she returns."

I didn't like feeling like I needed his permission but the truth was I did. Desperate to focus on something concrete, I turned to the woman who with that nose could only be his sister. She'd been watching our interaction quietly. "I'm sorry about your mom."

She smiled, her eyes tired. "If you really are her friend, you knew it was only a matter of time. That woman is a wild thing."

Conrad snorted. "I'm getting coffee. I'll be back."

Neither of us acknowledged him. "I didn't catch your name."

"Elizabeth." She held out her left hand. There was no wedding ring on it, but she wore a magnificent turquoise and silver bracelet. "And don't worry about my brother. He's all bark and no bite. He's just worried about mom."

"Me too. Did you see her before she went into surgery?"

"I'm afraid not. We arrived shortly before you. Mr. Samuelson from the nursing home was already here. He gave us the same information he gave you."

She pushed her hair back from her ears, and I noticed sea-blue, speckled earrings that matched her bracelet. The creative jewelry along with her crisp white shirt and expensive scarf marked her as Not from Around Here. "You live in Fargo, too?"

She laughed, and it sounded like dry stones tumbling down a hill, the laugh of a repentant smoker. "Not for a while. I live in Sedona, in Arizona. I own an art gallery. Don't tell my brother, but I brought some healing crystals to put near mom's bed."

I shrugged. It made no difference to me. What I needed was to distract my fear until Mrs. Berns returned. "How'd you end up in Sedona from Battle Lake?"

That laugh again. "Our farm was actually north of Underwood. When I graduated high school in the fifties, there weren't a lot of options for women. I didn't want to get married, be a secretary, teacher, or nurse, so I moved to Minneapolis and took some art classes. Turns out I'm a mediocre artist but a great businesswoman." Her eyes sparkled, and for the first time, I saw her resemblance to Mrs. Berns. "I used my connections from the art classes to gather the work of talented no-names, dug up some good investors, and launched a gallery in the Cities. When it was doing well enough, I moved it to Sedona, where they have no winter and lots of people who can afford art. Been there since the sixties. I only come home for emergencies."

I smiled politely, but my brain was mathing. "But Mrs. Berns got in her accident only a couple hours ago. How did you get here so quickly?"

Her eyes arched, and her resemblance to Mrs. Berns was replaced by her resemblance to her brother. "Same person, different emergency."

And that's when Mrs. Berns was wheeled into the room, flat on her back, eyes closed.

ELEVEN

MY FEET WERE ROOTED to the floor. Elizabeth gently led me to the side as two nurses wheeled in Mrs. Berns and positioned her bed parallel to Mrs. Skolen's, the curtain dividing them. A third nurse followed closely with an IV and monitor on wheels. All three of them had grim, distant smiles strapped to their faces.

The nurse who appeared to be in charge, a heavyset blonde, spoke loudly to Mrs. Berns, who had a bandaged head, a face full of purple and black bruises, and her leg propped up in a cast. "We're in your room now, honey. I know you're awake in there, so no use pretending. You're gonna be sore, but the sooner you're up and around, the sooner you'll start healing." She pressed a white cylinder into Mrs. Berns' hand, which looked as weak and light as a fallen bird. "If you start feeling pain, you just give this a click. It's your morphine drip."

My heart lightened, then soared. I knew what was happening! Mrs. Berns wasn't nearly as destroyed as she appeared. She was playing possum until the nurses left, and then she'd morphine drip herself into Timbuktu while watching *Judge Judy*, eating lime Jell-O, and crank-calling the rehab ward. It would be her dream vacation. I kept a straight face until the nurses were done with their bustling, and then I leaned toward my old friend, quiet so Elizabeth wouldn't hear. "You want to watch out with that drip. I've heard of people getting video-game thumb from pressing it too much."

Her eyes fluttered, and then opened, looking rheumy and unfocused. For the first time, I noticed that her skin was so thin it was almost translucent. A tear rolled down her cheek, and she asked, her voice scared, "Where am I?"

And that's when I remembered that nothing good lasts forever.

———

Fortunately, Mrs. Berns' skull was fully intact. Her doctor okayed her move out of ICU as soon as a regular hospital room became available. Mrs. Skolen was required to remain in ICU for at least twenty-four hours longer. Conrad and Elizabeth had rented two hotel rooms in town and returned to them after they'd seen Mrs. Berns settled in for the night. I refused to leave her side. If I was here, I could make sure she didn't have nightmares or get thirsty. I'd locked up the library as soon as Wohnt had slapped me with the news, and it could stay locked forever as far as I was concerned.

She was in and out of consciousness for the first few hours I was alone with her, heavily doped on meds and unable to find a restful sleep. I sang to her, a quiet hum. She'd have punched me for it if she was awake, but it was enough to finally guide her into a deeper sleep. Either that or she was so annoyed by it she knocked herself out.

As much as I didn't want to, once her breathing became deep and restful, I called Johnny to ask him to take care of Luna and Tiger Pop. He said all the right things and promised to come straight to the hospital afterward, but I'd convinced him that now wasn't the time, that Mrs. Berns needed quiet to recover. The tears were rolling down my cheeks when I told him, but I kept my voice even on the phone. I could only deal with one crisis at a time.

I guarded Mrs. Berns' sleep for a while, her chest rising and falling fitfully underneath the white bandages, her casted leg propped up in bed. The woman had saved my life, could spot a lie at a hundred yards, and made life more fun than it had any right to be. And with her eyes closed, she looked just like any little old lady with a few doddering years left in her. I glanced back at the phone, blurry through the tears, and considered that maybe I did need Johnny to get through tonight. *No*, I thought, resting my head on the side of her bed, *I can get through this alone.* It was the only way I knew how.

I couldn't stand the worrying any longer so replaced it with a prayer to every god I'd ever heard of, with an added plea to fairies, leprechauns, and four-leaf clovers, just in case. There's no coward like an agnostic who believes her best friend is knocking at death's door.

"How is she?"

I started. I hadn't heard the door open. "Bernard?"

He was walking funny, like his leg hurt him, and he had a glistening blue and green bruise on his left temple. "They said she was going to be fine."

"What happened to you?"

"I fell. How's the other woman? Freda, is that her name?"

He was anxious, repeatedly running his fingers through his hair and then shuffling them into his pockets to play with pieces of lint or whatever secrets they held. My antennae were up, alerted by his injuries and body language. Neither Conrad nor Elizabeth knew whose Dodge pickup Mrs. Berns had been driving, or where she and Freda had been going. A witness had spotted the vehicle overturned on

County Road 29 going east, Mrs. Berns behind the wheel, awake but without her seatbelt on and Freda next to her, belted in and unconscious. I took a stab. "You fall into a steering wheel?"

His eyes narrowed and his hands stilled. "What?"

"You drive a pickup?" The pieces were falling into place. Mrs. Berns was wild, but she wasn't stupid. She always used condoms, washed her hands after using the toilet, and wore her seatbelt.

His face went ashen, underscoring the ugly nature of his bruise. "I let her borrow the truck. I didn't know she was such an abdominal driver." He was backing toward the door.

I stood, the accumulated stress of the past twenty-four hours roaring toward my mouth. "You were driving that pickup when it got into the accident, weren't you? You unbuckled Mrs. Berns and pulled her behind the wheel and fled, didn't you?" My hands felt huge and meaty, itching to pound into something. I advanced, and Bernard cowered.

"Stop it."

My ears perked, and I swiveled to the bed. "Mrs. Berns?" She'd spoken only a handful of words since her surgery, and none of them were commands. "Did you say something, Mrs. Berns?"

Her eyes fluttered open and then focused. "A dumbass says what?"

"What?" I said.

She cackled, which immediately turned into a painful cough. "Damn ribs. They're broken you know, Bernard. Three of 'em. You get that driver's license same place you got your journalist's license? On the Interweb?"

He rushed to her side and grabbed her hand. I thought he was going to pour apologies, but instead he said, "Don't tell on me. Please. I don't want to go back to jail."

I shoved him to the side so I could get in close to her. "How are you feeling?"

"Like the prettiest boy in prison," she said, and then attempted another weak chortling. "No offense, Bernard."

"You shaved ten years off my life," I told her, relieved tears burning hot at the corners of my eyes.

"Think what it did to me." She fumbled for the bed adjuster. "How's Freda?"

I chose my words carefully. "She's pretty banged up, but she'll pull through. What were you three doing?"

Mrs. Berns' eyes twinkled, even if the rest of her couldn't. "Getting a marriage license."

I glanced quickly at Bernard, but he was stone-faced. "For whom?"

"For the two of us," he said defensively. "We're in love and we're going to espouse each other. On Halloween."

I fell heavily into the chair I'd pulled next to the bed. "How long have you known each other?"

"Almost a week, and shut up," Mrs. Berns said. "I'm tired. I need you to do something, and I don't have any extra juice to explain myself. You my friend?"

"Of course I am."

"Then listen. My beloved Bernard Mink and I are going to get married." He reached for her hand but she swatted him away. "But we can't get married if he's in jail. So you have to find out who murdered that bobber at the motel, and you have to keep quiet about who was driving the pickup."

"No way," I said. "First of all, since when do *you* want to get married? You're the one who said we'd stay single forever as a passive resistance, that if enough good women refused to get married, men would have to improve. You said the next generation could reap the rewards of our sacrifices."

"Changed my mind."

"For this?" I indicated the pork-bellied Mr. Mink, who had gone back to nervously running his hands through his hair and had added timid mustache twirling to the repertoire.

"Love is a capricious thing. Now shut the hell up. Are you in?" Her voice was feisty but her eyes were fading.

"Wait, how did you know the blogger was murdered?"

Mrs. Berns pointed at Bernard. "Heard it through the grapevine."

"And how does me finding the killer help Bernard?"

"It helps all three of us, pudding head, because we were all in Dead Body City, Minnesota, at the wrong time. It especially helps Bernard, however, as he has some past issues that might make the law treat him unkindly if they learned he was sleeping next to the room where his rival was hung."

"Rival?" I asked Bernard.

"Just a friendly opposition among newsmen," he said. "Nothing worth mentioning."

"Would Bob the blogger have called it friendly?"

He shrugged and then looked away to twirl his mustache like he was hoping to jumpstart an escape helicopter.

"Crap," I said, looking back at Mrs. Berns. "This is really what you want?"

She nodded, her eyes already closed.

"Fine." How do you refuse a woman you love in her hospital bed? And the fact of the matter was I'd been lying to myself about not caring who murdered Webber. Like an accidental vampire, I'd had my first taste of blood—or in my case, the thrill of solving a mystery—last May, and I was hooked, despite all my internal protestations to the opposite. Mrs. Berns was just giving me an excuse to do what I wanted to do anyway. "But only if you tell me why Conrad and Elizabeth were in Battle Lake."

"Tomorrow," she croaked, and then she drifted back into her drug haze.

TWELVE

Dwindling state funding had forced me to cut the Monday through Thursday library hours from 9 to 8 to 12 to 6. The decision had made me livid. The library wasn't a storehouse for books. It was the centerpiece of the community. Probably I should have let that anger drive my interest in government decisions. Instead, it was the discovery of a dead body and my pledge to Mrs. Berns that had me researching politics more deeply than I'd ever thought possible.

Taking advantage of the late opening of the library, I sat at one of the public computers, the guest list that I had pinched from the cleaning cart at my side. I'd dug it out of the garbage during a quick home pit stop on my way back from the hospital. I hadn't slept or eaten in going on thirty hours. I felt as fuzzy as a dishrag, but I had a plan. I was going to research all the guests who were at the motel the night of the alleged murder. Most people can be found online, even if we're not public figures, though I was willing to guess a fair number of the Saturday night guests had been in town for the debate, either on one of the politician's teams or a reporter. Then, I'd generate a list of possible suspects, putting Bernard Mink at the top. I wasn't going to break my promise to Mrs. Berns to exonerate Bernard of potential charges, but that didn't mean I was going to be an idiot, either. Even if he wasn't a murderer, he didn't feel like one of the good guys, and I wasn't letting my best friend go into anything blind.

After I'd narrowed the list, I'd suck in my pride and good sense and call Kennie to find out if she knew any more than she'd told me yesterday, or if she'd found out anything since then. Finally, I would be trying to track down the suspects, all of whom should still be in town if Deputy Wohnt had delivered to them the same message he'd given me about staying put, and see if any of them had a free moment to confess to murder.

If my scheme was a movie, it'd be more *Fools Rush In* than *A Star Is Born*, but it was all I had. So I set to work.

Room Number	Guest	Check in/Check out
1	Brett Lombardy	10/17-10/19
2	Nathan Froberg	10/17-10/19
3	Stephen Rudy	10/18-10/19
4	Robert Webber	10/17-10/18
5	James Durecki	10/18-10/19
6	Peter McGough	10/17-10/19
7	Jay Griffin	10/17-10/19
8	Duane Didier	10/17-10/18
9	Alex Pokof	10/17-10/20
10	Greg Hansen	10/12-10/19
11	Ryan Hansen	10/12-10/19
12	David Hansen-Aas	10/12-10/19
13	Melissa Hansen	10/12-10/19
14	Bernard Mink	10/17-10/19

15	Sarah Glokkmann	10/17-10/19
16	Karl Bachin	10/17-10/19
17	Arnold Swydecker	10/17-10/19
18	Grace Swinton	10/17-10/19
19	Glenn Vanderbrick	10/17-10/18*pm checkout
20	John Leeson	10/18-10/19

The room list showed that every room but two had been booked Saturday night: room 4, the room Webber had vacated on Friday, and room 19, the site of the dead body, which had "Glenn Vanderbrick" listed as occupant. Mr. Vanderbrick's departure date column had 10/18 with an asterisk next to it and the words "pm checkout" penciled in. That explained why room 19 was empty the next morning, but why hadn't room 4 been filled after Webber checked out? Between the debate and Octoberfest, the town had been packed for the weekend. With only two motels in town, I couldn't imagine there'd be a Saturday night vacancy to spare.

Humoring a hunch, I held the list up to the cold October sunshine and was rewarded—the date next to Bob Webber's name had a tiny blot on the bottom of the "8" that didn't let in light. I placed the list on the desktop and used the edge of my fingernail to scrape the white-out off the lower left edge of the "8" on 10/18, revealing that he had originally intended to check out on the 19th. Someone had blotted the sleek bottom of the nine and replaced it with a tiny circle in pen the same color. Had his date change been so abrupt that the hotel hadn't had time to reprint a list, or had someone tampered with the cleaning list, and if so, to what end? I didn't suppose I could call the motel to find out what their computer system said about the dates he'd booked, but I'd sure like to know.

Tabling what I couldn't address right now, I typed an alphabetical list of the twenty names so I didn't have to mess up the original list with scribbled notes. Ignoring the alphabetical order, I started with Glenn Vanderbrick, the most likely suspect by virtue of location, and quickly found that he was a blogger as well as an on-call political columnist for various Midwest newspapers. Scanning his blog page, I didn't see the thoroughness or sleek writing style of Webber's, but he was good enough. As an off bet, I did a site search on his page for the name "Bob Webber" and came across several articles they'd cowritten. I didn't know what that meant, that Webber had been killed in the room vacated by a coauthor, so I chose the direct route and sent Vanderbrick an e-mail explaining that I was a reporter from Battle Lake and would like to speak with him if he'd be so kind as to send me his phone number. I also included mine.

Returning to alphabetical order, I investigated Karl Bachin, whose room location between Glokkmann and Swydecker suggested he was a member of one of their campaigns. However, his two fame Googles consisted of his bowling team's second place trophy in a Southeastern Minnesota bowling tourney and his post to a listserv regarding his preference for Brewer's Best home beer brewing kits over True Blue Gold. A better online profile for an Octoberfest expert I could not have written. The next three names drew equal dead ends.

Glokkmann was the fifth name, and she understandably called out a whole slew of hits, the first couple pages of which I'd already read. A few deep blog postings hinted that Glokkmann was off her rocker, referring to her recent immigrant comment as well as statements she'd made about the baseless global warming scare being an anti-American conspiracy, but the only direct accusations I could find originated at the blog of Bob Webber. I perused his articles on Glokkmann more closely. In several pieces covering the alleged bribes she'd received from the oil industry, Webber cited her tax returns and her public campaign fund record as evidence of her illegal behavior, but when I cross-referenced those, I saw that while she had taken money from oil companies, she'd been up front about it. It might not be the height of ethics, but it didn't seem out of line with what every other politician was doing. Same with her voting on a bill that could have potentially helped her husband's business. If she thought it was a good bill for the state, she had a right to vote on it, regardless of how it benefitted her family.

When it came to her alleged drinking problem, though, Webber claimed to have several reliable sources who might in the future be willing to go on record stating that Glokkmann sometimes got so drunk during the day that she couldn't even be wheeled into the Congressional chambers, and several key votes had been missed as a result. Unfortunately, none of those "reliable sources" were willing to go on record at this time.

The only issue Webber had really pinned her on was taking two of her daughters to New York City on the state's dime. Glokkmann testified that she'd had to attend a conference and didn't know she wasn't allowed to bring her children. The issue had been scheduled to come before the House Ethics Committee last month, but Glokkmann sidestepped that by repaying the money and issuing a formal apology for her "honest mistake." So, even in the issue that she was likely guilty of, she came out smelling like a rose. In reading the article, I was drawn to a throw-away line mentioning that she and her husband had adopted or fostered eighteen children. Wow. I was stretching myself thin with a cat and a dog.

Based on what I knew, Glokkmann should be my biggest suspect in Webber's murder because she had the most substantial grind against him. But, the more I thought about it, the more I decided that made her the least likely killer. She'd be stupid to snuff the man who was publicly trying to take her down, and she struck me as cruel but not dumb. Back to square one, maybe one and a half. I returned to the list and in the range of the H's to the R's found a group at the motel for a family reunion, a couple who had just gotten married and, according to their travel blog, were hitting Midwest festivals for their honeymoon, Bernard Mink in the room right below the one where Webber had been found, and a slew of dead-ends.

I reached the S's and observed that Swinton and Swydecker were next to each other alphabetically. Their motel rooms were adjacent as well with Swinton in 18, which was the unused room I'd seen her enter yesterday morning. Swydecker was in 17. Why hadn't Glokkmann and Swinton gotten rooms side by side? Was that the room glitch I had seen her complaining about at the front desk the night I'd gone to meet Johnny? And had Swinton been in Glokkmann's room Saturday night, and that's why her room was unused? If so, had they been working on campaign strategy or on something more sinister? But Kennie had said Glokkmann and one of her staff had no alibi, so if they'd been together that night, they surely would have covered for each other.

A knock at the front door interrupted my train of thought, and I glanced up, annoyed. Couldn't a woman uncover a murderer in peace? At the other side of the door was Bad Brad, my ex, the man who had helped set the events in motion that had brought me to Battle Lake. Right about the time I'd decided my life was crap and I was drinking too much, I'd stumbled onto the neighbor's visiting niece playing a solo on his pink oboe. These are the crazy things you see when you spy on your boyfriend through a skylight. Choosing the passive-aggressive route, rather than confront him with the facts, I jacked his bike tires so they'd come off mid-journey and pointed west without saying goodbye. Unfortunately, Fate can find you anywhere. Brad and his band had ended up playing a gig in Battle Lake back in July and we'd accidentally reunited, him doofily and me kicking and screaming. Unfortunately, he felt right at home in Battle Lake and decided to stay. He'd talked most of his band into relocating with him.

Even though we now lived in the same tiny town, we didn't hang in the same circles. Actually, I didn't really hang anywhere but home and the library, which worked nifty when there are lots of people you want to avoid. I stormed over to the door, unlocked it, and yanked it open. "What?"

"Hey, babe." The brains had never been what had attracted me to him. In retrospect, I wasn't sure what had. "How's it hanging?"

"I'm really busy. Whaddya need?"

He shot his eyes over my shoulder. "Um, a book?"

"Gotta wait 'til we open." I let the door swing shut, locked it, and returned to my computer station. I worked steadily for five minutes before I realized he was still outside the door, a hangdog look on his face. I stomped back. "What?"

He pointed at the etched numbers on the door. "This says the library opened twenty-five minutes ago."

I hate trading in my anger for embarrassment, so I didn't bother. "Whatever," I said, leaning over to flip on the rest of the lights. "Knock yourself out."

I cleaned up my computer station, shuffling my meager notes so they were in order before stuffing them into my cloth purse, and I went about the business of running a library. Over the next hour people came and went, but Brad stayed. I mostly ignored him until it became grossly apparent he needed help. Then I ignored him for another ten minutes before approaching.

He glanced quickly at his feet, and the edges of his face pinked. This from the man who when we were dating used the toilet with the bathroom door open so he could watch the TV in the other room. I had to admit I was intrigued. "You don't need to be embarrassed," I said. "Reading is nothing to be ashamed of."

"I need to find a book that explains how to get rid of eyelash crabs." He was talking so fast that it came out as one long word.

"Oh," I said. "I stand corrected."

"Don't judge me, Mira."

Judge him? That would have taken my focus away from laughing. Maybe all three Fates weren't lined against me. I stepped back another five feet. "You should probably just go to the doctor."

"I hate needles."

I considered conjecturing about the size of the syringe the doctor would likely use to eradicate the bugs but thought better of it. Now was a good time as any to put some quarters toward the red ink of my karma. "The doctor won't use needles."

Either his eyes lit up or the crabs were sending me an SOS. "Really? You've had eyelash crabs before?"

"I don't even know how you get … never mind. You just go to the doctor, they rinse off your eyelashes with a special liquid, and you're all better. No worries." I actually had no idea how a doctor would address this particular situation but I wanted Brad to go away.

"I don't know how to thank you, Mir." He leaned in to give me a hug and I lunged for one of the newspaper holders, pointing it toward him like a sword.

"No thanks necessary."

"Okay, then. I better get to the doctor."

"Okay then."

He smiled again, and I recognized it as his flirtatious smile, the one that preceded him asking me if I wanted to ride the baloney pony. "You sure look good."

Like a cockroach that can ambulate without its head, Brad could still flirt while carrying a load of face lice. "Leave."

He didn't have the brains to be hurt. He nodded as if I'd told him it looked like rain today and then started on a new conversational track. "Hey, Not With My Horse is playing in town tonight. You should come check us out. We've gotten four new gigs out of our blazing Octoberfest performance. Did you see us? We rocked that jam!"

"That's awesome. Bye."

"And we even had cute groupies this time. You shoulda been there! I got with a hot little number between sets. Somebody famous."

Again, he lit my curiosity against its will. "Somebody famous from Battle Lake?"

"Just in town for a coupla nights," he said coyly. "Wanna guess who?"

"Nope."

"She's connected to politics."

Cripes. It was probably Kennie Rogers. It for *sure* wasn't Sarah Glokkmann. Maybe Swinton? She seemed too high class for a pre-encore one-nighter with a polka-fusion singer, but I didn't know any other politics-affiliated women in town. "Don't care. And you should tell her you've got critters setting up shop on your face."

He seemed to consider and then discard this. "Thanks again for your help. You know where to find me if you need me."

"Not gonna happen."

He nodded conspiratorially, as if my words were code for something else, and headed out to, I could only hope, get the biggest shot in the butt of his life. I took advantage of the lull in the library to call Kennie. Might as well group my unpleasant tasks.

"Hello, Bronze and Bond. How may we make all your dreams come true?"

"Hi, Kennie. It's me. I have a couple questions."

"Hmm. Well who needs whom now?"

Which is precisely why I'd dreaded this call. "Look, I'll help you out tomorrow. I promise. In exchange, I need you to answer a few questions. Deal?"

I heard the sound of a nail file at work. "We'll see. What're the questions?"

"First one: you said that Glokkmann didn't have an alibi for Saturday night, right?"

Kennie exhaled. "Not exactly. That little cookie has always been a squirmy one. She says she was at the motel, in her room, from ten o'clock that night on. Thing is, there's no one to corroborate her story. She was sharing her room with one of her daughters, who was out partying with a band all night."

The shortest distance between two points is a line. "How old's her daughter?"

"I dunno. Twenties I suppose."

Bingo. Bet I just discovered Brad's political liaison. "Are Glokkmann and her daughter still in town?"

"They are, and so are her people. And Swydecker. Deputy Wohnt told them it would be in their best interest to remain in our fair city." She sighed. "Doesn't he look great? That man has put on weight in all the right places since he left."

I ignored her. "So Glokkmann and her crew and Swydecker and his crew are in town indefinitely but everyone else in the motel was sent on their way?"

"Yes and no. Swydecker doesn't have a crew. But otherwise, you got it."

"So those two are the main suspects in Webber's murder?" I circled their names in my notebook and drew unhappy faces next to them.

"Not sure. The Deputy and I don't share all our information."

"But you're the Chief!"

She purred. "I certainly am, but a smart woman knows to let a man feel like he's in charge." She tried to switch subjects. "Have you seen all the national news reporters in town? Bronze and Bond is going to be a huge success."

"What's Swydecker's alibi?"

"I'll tell you after you help me spray-tan strangers."

I groaned. "Can't you tell me now?"

"And risk you not showing? No way. Free help is hard to come by."

"You said I'd make $250 an hour!"

"No, I asked you if you *wanted* to make $250 an hour. Completely different than offering you $250 an hour. One is a commitment, and the other is small talk. See you tomorrow at 6:00!" And she hung up.

Agh. No use worrying about what I couldn't change. I channeled my frustration into researching Bernard Mink, my last total unknown. I first located a series of *Register* articles he'd written. He didn't seem to have a beat, covering sports, local news, and community events equally. More interesting than the articles he'd written were the ones he appeared in. They weren't news stories so much as police logs, and I unearthed two of them, one from three years ago and one posted the previous month. The oldest blotter entry:

Police were called to a Lincoln Street residence on a report of domestic dispute. Officers arrived to find Fergus Falls residents Bernard Mink, age fifty-three, and Andrea Lang, age forty-two, arguing over meatballs. Mr. Mink was charged with fifth-degree assault for threatening to choke Ms. Lang with a Crockpot power cord and fourth degree assault for resisting arrest. Ms. Lang left with the meatballs.

And the most recent:

Police were called to a Lincoln Street residence on a report of domestic dispute. When officers arrived, they discovered a belligerent Bernard Mink, Fergus Falls resident, age fifty-six, in a physical altercation with Pelican Rapids resident Claude Wayne, age thirty-two. Mr. Wayne claimed he was a neighbor who'd interceded in a physical fight between Mr. Mink and Roberta Kennedy, Fergus Falls resident, age sixty-three. Ms. Kennedy declined to press charges. Mr. Mink was charged with third-degree assault.

The police logs left my hands shaking. They painted a portrait of Bernard as an abusive creep. I had figured I would find something like this, but I didn't want to be right. I had to tell Mrs. Berns, but how?

THIRTEEN

I STRODE INTO MRS. Berns' hospital room and was happy to find that her family wasn't around. "Here." I held out the pumpkin-and-spice colored mums I'd bought for her, trying not to wince at the sight of her harsh bruises. "How're you doing?"

She shushed me and pointed at the TV. The evenings news was on, and if my eyes weren't deceiving me, this national news station's cameras were panning downtown Battle Lake. "And it's here that the campaigns of Representative Sarah Glokkmann and her challenger, Arnold Swydecker, took a precarious turn." The camera found the face of the commentator and widened slightly to include an appropriately somber-looking Glokkmann.

"Representative Glokkmann, can you comment on the death of Bob Webber, the man behind *The Body Politic*?"

"It's terribly sad, Craig. This whole town is shook up about it. My staff tells me it appears to be suicide. He must have been a desperate man."

The commentator nodded sagely. "There's been some talk that this was a murder."

Glokkmann looked shocked. "Well, I'll leave the investigative work to the police force."

The reporter tightened his lips. "Will this unfortunate tragedy affect your campaign?"

"I'm always saddened by an early death, but I didn't know Mr. Webber personally. My condolences go out to his friends and family. In the meanwhile, I have a job as a representative of Minnesota, and I have a duty to fulfill. I will fulfill it."

"Thank you. I'm Craig Clutch, live from Battle Lake, Minnesota."

I stared at the image of Glokkmann appearing properly sad but not weak. She was a polished act, and I became aware that I needed to speak with her, and soon. Swydecker, too. They wouldn't be in town for much longer, and I had a strong hunch that one of them knew exactly who'd killed Bob Webber.

"That woman is as slick as pirate snot, isn't she?" Mrs. Berns flipped off the TV.

"I didn't know you watched that channel."

"Gotta get my laughs somewhere."

I smiled. "You never answered me from before. How're you feeling?"

"That's a stupid question. My face is purple, my leg is broken, and my ribs are cracked. I'm feeling like a half-eaten lobster. They tell me I get out Wednesday, though, so you better come pick me up."

"Really? That soon?"

"Insurance doesn't want to pay to keep an old lady around. They say the rehab facilities at the Sunset will be enough. You bring me any wine with those flowers?"

"Sorry. Doctor's orders. You must have much better stuff here anyhow."

She shook her head sadly. "Used to, but I don't any longer. Got my morphine privileges revoked yesterday. Seems the hospital staff has a different definition of 'as needed' than I do. So tell me what you know about who killed the bobber."

"Blogger. And first you gotta tell me why Elizabeth was in town, remember?"

"Blogger to you too." She sighed dramatically and flattened her bedspread. "Fine. You know that it's Conrad's fault I was checked into a nursing home a few years back, right?"

I nodded.

"Well, that same bug has bit him again. Somebody told somebody about our wild antics at the State Fair, and it got back to him. He's putting his foot down."

"*Our* wild antics?"

"I'm an old lady. You're going to put all this on my shoulders?"

I rolled my eyes and got back on topic. "But that doesn't make any sense. You're already in a nursing home. What more can he do?"

She handed me a brochure from her nightstand. "Shady Acres Retirement Home" was emblazoned across the top. I flipped it open. It looked like a bucolic place. "I haven't heard of this one. Where's it at?"

"South of the Cities. And it's a maximum security place for elderly patients with dementia. He wants me declared mentally incompetent and shipped off for my own safety. His words."

"Noooo!"

She furrowed her brow. "He needs at least two family signatures on the commitment form, which is why Elizabeth flew up. She wanted to see firsthand if I was as loony as Conrad was saying."

I thought back. "That's why you were wearing granny clothes last time I saw you at the Sunset?"

"Among other things, like going to church regularly and getting a marriage license I didn't intend to use to prove I'm stable. Told my kids I'd been dating Bernard for a year. We were going to get the license and be engaged long enough for Conrad to lose interest in me and find some other life to ruin. The plan had been working right up until the car accident. Now Elizabeth is back on the fence. She says she believes in personal freedom but doesn't know if I'm capable of making the best decisions for myself anymore."

"Wow." I dropped heavily into the bedside chair. "You did a crap job raising those kids."

"You're telling me."

"So what're we going to do?"

"*I'm* going to get married."

"What?" The printouts of Bernard's criminal past were burning through my purse. "Bernard is a dunce."

"Exactly." She fiddled with a gaudy glass ring on her finger. "Dumb enough to marry me and do everything I say. He'd be my legal guardian, even if my traitor children managed to declare me incompetent. Of course, if Bernard murdered the bobber, it's all over for me. He'll go to jail and my kids'll ship me off to old lady prison. You'll never see me again."

"Don't be so dramatic," I said, unwilling to admit how hard my heart had constricted at her words. "I'm sure there's another way. I'll talk to Elizabeth."

"Do what you want as long as you do what you promised: find out who killed the man in the motel. What have you uncovered so far?"

I wrinkled my forehead. "I don't know any more about that than I did last time I saw you."

"Have you asked that Glokkmann if she did it? She looks like a bad sort."

"I'll talk to her this week." I was stalling. I knew I should tell Mrs. Berns about Bernard, but I didn't want to increase her stress right now. I'd have to find a different way to keep her out of the maximum security home so she wouldn't have to marry him. How's Freda?"

Mrs. Berns grew serious. "She's out of ICU, but she'll be in the hospital a little longer. You should visit her before you go. She doesn't get many visitors. Her sister and most of her friends are too old to drive."

"Will do," I said. I was about to tell her I'd had flowers delivered to Freda's room on my way up when my attention was arrested by one of the top five most annoying sounds in the world: someone saying "knock knock" rather than actually knocking.

"Anybody home?" And in peeked Tanya Ingebretson, whom I hadn't seen since the debate, where she'd been the only local besides me. She disliked Mrs. Berns for the same reasons she hated me, so seeing her in the hospital room was puzzling.

Mrs. Berns tilted her bed so she was sitting upright. "Tanya! Thank you so much for coming. I wasn't sure you would."

I switched my surprise from Tanya to Mrs. Berns. I'd never heard her so polite in her life. I surreptitiously checked to make sure she wasn't hiding a morphine drip after all.

She glared at me, but out of sight of Tanya. "Mira, you must know Tanya Ingebretson. She does so much good for Battle Lake."

"Surely I must," I said sarcastically, reaching my hand out to Tanya. She slipped a business card into it: "Tanya Ingebretson, Life Coach," written in swirly girl letters.

"I'm board certified."

"What board?" I asked. A heady dose of expensive perfume wafted up from the card.

"The Global Life Accreditation Bureau. If you ever want to take charge of your life, give me a call." She turned her attention to Mrs. Berns. "I have to say I was surprised to receive your message. You of all people! But I suppose it makes sense because who needs more help than those who have fallen the farthest from The Light?"

I could hear the capital letters. And see them on the card I was still holding: Let Her Walk with You to The Light. "Where does one go to school to learn to be a life coach?"

She gave me a brittle smile. She was used to naysayers. "I went to the school of life, honey."

"Hmm. Maybe I should be a life coach."

"You can." She didn't sound convinced. "You have to practice for two years to be certified, not have any ethical violations, and pass a ten-point life coach multiple-choice test with a score of 70 percent or higher to be board certified."

She said it like it wasn't the stupidest thing I'd ever heard. "Mrs. Berns, what'd you call Tanya about?"

Mrs. Berns hid the grin that had been fed by my light bickering with Tanya. "To get my life in order, of course. I've made many mistakes"—here Tanya nodded in profound agreement—"and it's time for changes. I want to live in The Light."

I rolled my eyes. I was sure that Tanya was in the picture for the same reason as Bernard Mink and the granny pants, but that didn't make fake Mrs. Berns any easier to swallow. On an up note, however, I was glad she hadn't put all her buns in the Bernard Mink basket. "I think I'll visit Freda and leave you two to your business. Call me if you need anything."

"Of course, Mira," Mrs. Berns said, in a voice so cultured it made my ears hurt. "And I'd love to treat you to dinner at Stella's after you drive me home from the hospital on Wednesday. Is that proposition acceptable?"

"Yes, most certainly." I ducked out as quickly as I could and tracked down Freda. Her bruises colored her as brightly as an Easter egg, and one eye was still swollen shut, but she was thrilled by the company. We shared dinner, me eating a turkey and cheese sandwich that was surprisingly good for hospital food until I remembered it was my first solid food in nearly two days. I must have inhaled it because Freda offered me her applesauce. She tried to be good company but was still in a lot of pain. The doctors had told her they wouldn't know until the end of the week if she'd be able to walk without help, but her attitude was as sunny as spring. I promised to stop by to visit on Wednesday when I picked up Mrs. Berns.

My next and final stop before reuniting with my beloved bed was the Old Brick Inn to find out if Brad had, in fact, slept with Sarah Glokkmann's daughter on Saturday night. If he had, their stories didn't jibe. He'd told me they'd only bumped uglies between sets, but Kennie'd said that Glokkmann's daughter couldn't offer her mom an alibi because she was out with a band all night. I wanted to know which version was true.

By the time I arrived at the busy bar, it was past ten o'clock at night and I was so tired that I was hallucinating. I exited the car into a night that was cool enough for a medium jacket and smelled as clean as frost and woodsmoke. A lonely wind rustled through the dried leaves still clinging to trees. It was the perfect weather for curling up in a quilt. I hadn't slept in my own bed since Friday night, and had logged six total hours of sleep since then. The sandwich seemed to be staying down fine, but my stomach wasn't yet at 100 percent. I'd make this quick.

It was unusual to find a live band in town playing on a Monday night, so either Brad was correct that Not With My Horse's October-fest gig had increased their following or all the news crews in town didn't have anything better to do. I certainly didn't recognize most of the people seated in the darkly-lit main room, but bars tend to create their own small communities, and I'd never frequented this one much. The band had launched into a techno cover of "Delta Dawn" just as I entered. Disappointed that I hadn't caught them on a break, I squeezed up to the bar and ordered a club soda.

Somebody tapped my arm "You here to see the band?"

I turned, immediately defensive, and then did a double take. The woman who'd addressed me was Grace Swinton, Glokkmann's handler. "What?" I'd heard her, but I used the noise of the band as a cover to decide what I wanted to ask. I hadn't planned on running into Glokkmann or a member of her entourage.

She indicated my club soda and raised her voice. "Not many reasons to come to a bar if you're not going to drink."

I took a swig. "Just needed to get out of the house. You?"

She appeared thoughtful for a moment, and then held up her drink. It was dark, and I recognized the smell of whiskey, at least a double shot. "Me too. Just needed to get out of the house."

I considered lying, but up close, she seemed defenseless. The dim lighting colored her hair like mud, and she had worry lines feathering her eyes and mouth. I chose the straight route. "You're in town with the representative, aren't you?"

Her eyes flashed and she turned away.

"I'm sorry. It's just that I saw you at the news conference Saturday morning. This must be a stressful time for you."

She took a deep pull off her sweating glass. "Yeah."

"Can I buy you another?"

She shrugged. "What the hell."

Brad screamed into his back-up singer microphone like a neutered cat and we both temporarily glanced his way. I ordered her another and worked at small talk. "He's good looking, isn't he?" I indicated Brad, who had the poor timing to be humping the drum set, balancing his bass over his head.

"He looks like a dick."

Dang she was growing on me. "He is. I used to date him. He cheated on me."

She squinted her eyes in his direction, looking for what I must have seen in him. Good luck with that. "He is pretty hot, actually. But why doesn't he have any eyebrows?"

I swiveled in my seat to follow her gaze. I squinted my eyes, too, and had to agree with her analysis of his appearance. "He had face bugs."

She nodded as if that was the most normal thing in the world.

"Are you okay?" I asked. "You look kinda sad."

"Long weekend."

"I heard." I put all my chips on the table. "I work for the newspaper in town. Somebody was murdered, somebody your boss didn't like, and she doesn't have an alibi for the night he was offed. It doesn't look good."

She surprised me with a guffaw. "This isn't *Murder She Wrote*, you know." The smile lit her face like a thousand fireflies. "The death is sad, but Sarah isn't tied to it at all. We're staying in town a few extra days so she can listen to the voices of her constituents and bring them back to Congress."

I had to give her points for staying on message. "What about Swy-decker? Does he have an alibi?"

She grew tightlipped. "I can't speak for him."

"Fair enough." It made sense that she wouldn't defend her boss' opponent. Did it make equal sense that she wouldn't take an opportunity to badmouth him? Depended on her ethics.

"So the representative will be in town through Thursday? Friday?"

She stood and swayed slightly. "I think I've said more than enough. And it looks like your ex wants you. Good night."

She wove her way through the crowd and left with her drink still in hand. Not so legal. I hoped she was walking the four blocks back to the motel.

"Mira! You came."

Brad was upon me. His lack of eyebrows and eyelashes made him appear scared, or inquisitive. Or like a naked mole rat. "You visit the doctor?"

"Yeah, and you were right. No shot." He held his hands wide to indicate his pleasure with this outcome. "Whaddyou think of the band? We're on fire tonight."

"You've never sounded better," I said honestly. "Say, while I'm here, quick question. That Glokkmann chick you slept with during your show Saturday night, what was her name again?"

"Oh, Kenya?"

I snapped my fingers. "Yes! That's right. Kenya Glokkmann. You guys still seeing each other?"

He sidled a little closer. Through closed lips, I tried to emit a high whining noise to deter bug migration onto my person.

"You want your place back in my life?"

"You're a hard guy to forget, Brad. So, are you and Kenya an item?"

He turned away momentarily to accept a drink from a star-struck brunette, and I wondered if that's how I'd looked when I'd first approached him after a show at First Ave. I made a note to track her down on my way out and tell her that just this morning he'd told me he had crabs.

"Naw," he said, watching the brunette strut away. "Not dating. Just a little poke in the hay now and again while she's in town."

He nudged me like we shared a secret and was immediately distracted by another attractive woman strolling past. With his attention elsewhere, I grabbed a nearly empty drink and poured it where he'd touched me, figuring the alcohol would kill any critters the doctor had missed. "Did she stay for the after party on Saturday night?"

"Nope. I noticed her backstage when we de-staged to let Leif do his extended accordion solo. I was on her as soon as I spotted her. I romanced her like there was no tomorrow, and then I sent her on her way before the encore but after I'd pulled out all the stops. You remember all the stops?"

I did. Pulling out all of them took five minutes, less if there was music with a steady drum beat. "So you two didn't even hang out after the show? Just a quickie during it?"

"Who said it was quick?"

I gave him the stink eye and he had the decency to look abashed. "Fine. Yeah. Just a one-off between sets."

"Any idea where she went after that?"

"No idea. I can tell you she wasn't at the after party but she is still in town. I bet I get fifteen calls a day from her. She's got it bad."

I looked around. "She here now?"

"No, but she said she's crashing later."

"So why not start something more permanent with her? You like her?"

He patted his chest. "In the Cities, I was a little fish. Here, I'm King Walleye. The ladies can't get enough of this rock star, and I don't intend to be bogged down by a single filly when I could run with the herd. Speaking of, you sticking around for the second set?"

I wondered if he could hear my teeth grinding. "Is the Pope Lutheran?"

He smiled happily and gave me the thumbs up, even though we were standing within inches of each other. I was scouring for the quickest way to excuse myself when I caught a familiar face on the other side of the bar. It was Johnny, scanning the crowd. My heart puckered. I dropped to my knees before his eyes landed on me and whispered up toward Brad. "Cover me. I gotta get outta here."

"Dude, what's up? Or should I say, what's down?" He smiled crookedly at his own joke.

"Not your worry. Just walk that way." I pointed at the exit opposite the door Johnny had entered and commanded Brad to walk at the same pace I was crawling so he could shield me from view.

For once in his life, Brad listened to me. He made his own sweet way to the door, though, stopping to high five fans and make small talk. When I was within dashing distance, I stood and made for the exit. I thought I heard someone call my name but stopped only long enough to whisper, "The bass player of the band gave me crabs!" to a group of women near the door. They nodded vigorously. I'd have to trust that the news would find its back to the innocent-looking brunette who'd bought Brad a drink.

On the ride home, I fought gravity to keep my gritty eyes open. I was running on fumes, aware that my lack of sleep was making me a poor driver. I wanted to speed, but I kept it slow. Thankfully, no deer jumped out at me, and I made it home unaccosted. I dragged my feet into the house, fighting the pull of my bed long enough to apologize to, feed, and water Luna and Tiger Pop. Once I knew they were taken care of, I crawled into my bedroom, hot tears wetting my eyes as I took in the beautiful sight of my soft, big, safe bed. I ditched my clothes and crawled under the fluffy quilt, nestling in like a baby bird. I was asleep before my eyes closed.

FOURTEEN

THIS TIME THE SCREAM that woke me was my own. I lurched into an upright position, my heart punching out of my chest. Luna was whining next to my bed, her ears back and tail wagging nervously. I automatically reached out to soothe her and then scanned the room for Tiger Pop. I was terrified, and I only got this scared when someone I cared about was threatened. There he was, balled up at the foot of my bed, unconcerned about my odd behavior. I petted him too, and he stretched so far he grew extra bones. The sun was promising to rise, and everything in my room seemed in its place. What had woken me? I lay back down and shut my eyes, and it slammed back.

Cold, waxy white skin, half-lidded dead eyes staring at me, lips pulled back in a pained rictus as he was forced to the other side without reporting his final, most important story. Bob Webber's bloodless, wasted face. I'd seen a gravedigger's share of dead bodies the last few months, and I'd grown callous about them. Or at least I wanted to believe I had. I'd stared at Webber dead on the floor as if he were a cut of meat at the grocer, distasteful but not earth-shaking. I'd walked away, sure I was unaffected. And I'd hardly slept since then. Only in the relaxation of REM did all the horror of his death wash over me. The poor man had been murdered, and his ghost had yet to see justice. He deserved better than that. Everyone did.

Afraid to go back to sleep, I crawled out of bed far too early. Pulling on pants, a T-shirt and a coat, I stepped outside into the brisk morning air. My breath came out in tiny cumulous clouds. Tiger Pop and Luna followed me, which had been my intention, and I gave them both a long overdue brushing. Luna was mostly German shepherd and her thick gold and black hair grew matted without regular tending. The monotonous activity usually relaxed both of us, but its magic didn't work this time. I tugged too hard and couldn't find a rhythm. Luna, sensing my unease, nipped at me. I wanted to pinch back.

Giving up on the brushing, I went back into the house and checked the interior temperature: 58 degrees. That had been perfect for sleeping under a thick comforter, but I needed more now that I was up and about. I pushed the thermostat to 68 and tried to relax at the soothing sound of the furnace kicking in. Standing in the central room of the open floor plan house, I examined my surroundings. My sink was free of dishes and my house clean but for dust. I vacuumed anyway to freshen the carpet and took the feather duster to the big open areas. None of it worked. I felt haunted.

Even the plants couldn't save me. I watered them, noting that the knobby baby orange had almost doubled in size. That made it as big as a pecan instead of an acorn, which wasn't a huge accomplishment unless you loved plants. My spices were working equally hard, and I let the fresh and pungent smell of their growth embrace me, but I couldn't shake the cold exhale of death on the back of my neck.

And that's when I realized I was ravenous. Striding to the fridge, I pulled out my last three eggs, a can of refried beans, an avocado that was nicely green-black on the outside and soft, two slices of sprouted grain sesame bread, and a jar of hot habañero salsa. I cooked the eggs over medium and cut the avocado in half, spearing the pit with the long end of my knife so I could pluck it out with a flick of my wrist. I sliced the green meat into five long sections on each half, scooped out the slices, and laid them in a fan on my plate before salting and peppering them. I opened the can of beans, heating half in the microwave and putting the other half in the fridge. The bread I popped into the toaster. When the microwave dinged, I yanked out the beans and spread them on my plate and slid the eggs on top, salting the works before liberally dousing it with salsa. The toast popped up and I buttered it, trying not to drool. At this point, my hands were shaking, either with a lack of proper nutrition or anticipation. A tall glass of half vanilla and half chocolate rice milk at my side, I dug in, not bothering to breathe or look up until there was nothing but faint smears on my plate to remind me that food had ever been there.

And when it was gone, I felt sick to my stomach. It was Bob Webber's jacket that I kept going back to, the sad worn coat that was the best he could do. "Who killed him?" I asked my animals. "Who killed him and why does it feel like they're not done yet?"

Luna thumped her tail and whined. I reassured her with a scratch behind the ears and popped in the shower. I was pretty sure my breakfast was visibly moving through my stomach like a rabbit in a snake's gut, so I kept my eyes raised. By the time I was dressed and my hair dry, it was 8:00 a.m., a perfectly reasonable time to travel to the Big Chief Motor Lodge and find out if the candidates wanted to talk to the local news.

It was early on a Tuesday for a city, maybe, but a farm town gets up with the sun, even after there aren't many farmers left. A steady stream of cars and pickups cruised down Lake Street, stopping in front of the Village Apothecary or parking so their owners could run in to the post office, waving hello to familiar faces on the way. The two places in town that served breakfast, the Shoreline and Turtle Stew, were full to the top. The parking lot at the Big Chief was thinner than it had been this weekend, but it still contained almost a dozen cars.

I wasn't sure if Glokkmann and Swydecker would be in their same rooms as Saturday night, but it seemed a reasonable place to start. I stopped in front of room 17 because it was nearest the stairs and knocked. And knocked again. I was about to give up when a brisk voice on the other side asked, "Who is it?"

I stared into my end of the peephole struggling to exude sweetness. "My name's Mira. I'm a local."

Hesitation from the other side, followed by a reluctant opening of the door. "Which news station? CBS? NBC? Just tell me you're not from Fox."

I held up my hands to show they were empty of recording devices. "None of the above. I really do live in Battle Lake."

"Then what do you want?" His voice was more perplexed than gruff. He was wearing a crisp white button-down shirt open at the collar, gray slacks with a black belt, and black shoes. He looked like he'd been up for a while. Swydecker's room also looked clean except for papers spread out over his unmade bed. He followed my gaze. "Sorry. Not expecting company."

"That's okay. I should tell you up front that I am a reporter."

He stiffened.

"But that's not why I'm here. A friend of mine is sort of caught up in the fallout of the murder, and I'm trying to help her. I was hoping I could ask you a few questions off the record?"

His right hand went to his left to fiddle with a piece of jewelry that wasn't there. I noted the faint tan line on his empty ring finger and filed that away. His marital problems did not concern me. "Why not? Haven't got anything to lose, have I?" He smiled. It took some effort. He led me over to the small round table by his TV and mini fridge. "Coffee? I'm afraid the pot only makes one cup at a time, but I've already had more than my share."

"No thanks. Coffee makes me jumpy."

"You should try being a murder suspect." He laughed, but it didn't touch his eyes.

"No one thinks you did it," I said. "I've been watching the news."

"Doesn't matter. Once you get connected to something like this, your political career is finished."

"Representative Glokkmann seems to be making the most of it."

"You sure you don't want coffee?" I shook my head, and he helped himself to the pot. He was right. It barely filled one Styrofoam cup. He added powdered creamer and two packets of sugar and started another pot brewing. I noticed he had a box of single-serving ground coffee bean packets. I also observed that he hadn't taken my bait. I changed the subject.

"Did you hear anything the night of the murder?"

He sipped the coffee like it was bitter. "Damn, what I wouldn't give for a good cup of joe. No, I was at the Octoberfest celebration until about 9 o'clock, and then I came back to my room."

"Alone?"

He raised his eyebrows. "I didn't bring any of my staffers to town with me. We're a lean bunch, anyhow. I don't accept corporate donations, which means I don't have extra cash lying around. I have wonderful volunteers, but they deserved a day off. The debate was to be short and sweet. So yes, I came here alone and I went straight to bed.

Didn't hear anything until the police sirens the next morning." His voice sounded defensive. He'd probably had to recite these words countless times the last two days.

"Why'd you get into politics?" The question wasn't on my list, but he seemed so normal and nice that I had to ask.

He chuckled ruefully. "Doesn't seem like my best idea right about now, does it? But I raised my kids to believe that they have to be the change they want to see in the world." He shrugged. "It was about time I lived up to that."

I bobbed my head toward his empty ring finger. "You're married?"

He moved his right hand to cover his left. "I am. How is this related to the murder?"

"Sorry," I said. "Did you know Bob Webber, the man who was murdered?"

"Just through the campaign trail. He was a stand-up man, the last of a dying breed of investigative reporters. He left a lucrative newspaper job because he was tired of reporting superficial stories, and he started his blog. I don't know that he'd ever get rich off of it, but he was making enough to get by through advertising. At least that's what he told me the one time I sat down with him for an interview a week or two ago. We were in my hometown, Detroit Lakes."

"He ever write any other articles on you, besides that one interview?"

"Several. I'm happy to report they were all positive. His work was a huge help to my campaign."

"Less of a help to Representative Glokkmann's campaign?"

"Is there anything more? I have some work to be getting to."

Why wouldn't he say anything bad about Glokkmann? Didn't he realize this was politics? "No, thank you. You've been very helpful."

I stood, and he followed suit, walking me to the door. "I hope for your friend's sake that they find the killer soon," he said.

"And I hope the same, for your sake."

He smiled sadly. "I think I'm already done in."

"I hope not." I meant it. He just about had the door closed when a thought struck me. "Mr. Swydecker!"

He reopened the door. "Yes?"

"I gotta know. When you were in public education? Were you a band teacher?"

He smiled, the first one I'd seen that reached his eyes. They made the corners wrinkle, and for the first time, I noticed his eyes were as blue and honest as Johnny's. "No. History."

FIFTEEN

I LEFT HIS ROOM feeling tremendously glum, and I wasn't sure why. Swydecker had filled in the blanks I'd had, and if that man was a murderer, I was a monkey's uncle. Something felt a little off with him, but I didn't sense it was about Webber's murder, other than a natural human sadness at violent death. I shrugged it off and continued down the second-floor walkway to Glokkmann's room. The response was much quicker. In fact, I met Grace Swinton coming out before I even knocked, her arms overflowing with papers, wearing dark sunglasses.

"Sorry," she said. "Didn't see you." She moved to the side and was about to continue down the stairs.

"Hangover?" I asked.

She tilted her chin so she could look at me over the top of her sunglasses. "Thought you looked familiar. You're that woman from the bar last night, the one who used to date the bass player."

"Guilty," I said. "But in my defense, I was a lot younger when we dated." In dog years.

She smiled. "You don't owe me an explanation. Are you here to interview the representative?"

"Sure," I said, making it up on the spot. "My editor would like to run a whole issue on modern politics with a special feature on the representative and her opponent." I couldn't get sued for lying, could I?

"That would be wonderful!"

"I'll just need her schedule while she's in town, so I can, you know, cover her events."

Grace paused for a moment, and I could tell she was trying to gauge me on her bullshit-meter. I must have passed because she said, "Follow me. I have to get these to the Representative right away. We can walk and talk."

I did follow her and even helped her to schlep some of the papers the five blocks to the main part of town. I spotted a commotion ahead. "What's going on?"

"As I told you last night, Sarah intends to make the most of her time in Battle Lake. She'll be speaking at the Kute Klips this morning and then will be meeting with voters at the Fortune Café for lunch."

My stomach rumbled at the mention of the Fortune. It was a wonderful coffee shop, bakery, used bookstore, and public computer space owned by two good friends of mine. They served an olive cream cheese that would make a dead man weep. I took my current fixation on food as a good sign. "Kute Klips is pretty small, isn't it? Where will she stand?"

We rounded the corner, and there hovered my answer. Kute Klips was a popular salon on the second story of a building zoned for business. It rested on top of Bill's Nonprofit Massage, and out front, it had an ornate balcony that I'd always assumed was decorative. That is, until I saw Sarah Glokkmann perched on it, beaming to reporters like Evita on the terrace of the Casa Rosada.

"There she is." Glokkmann spoke imperiously, pointing down at Grace. "She'll distribute the talking points."

I helped Grace dispense the handouts to the gathered press, maybe a dozen people from national and local news, four with cameras. There had been many more here yesterday, so some other story must currently be capturing the public's interest. A black-and-blue Bernard Mink was one of the reporters. He pretended not to know me when I handed him a sheet, and I scowled at him. I still didn't have a concrete plan for dealing with him, but deal with him I would.

When everyone present had a handout, Grace indicated for me to follow her up the stairs that clung to the outside of the building and into the beauty parlor. The smell on the second floor reminded me of the chemical pungency of the home permanents I'd begged my mom to give me in junior high. Salon perm? No, Ogilvie.

All four chairs in the beauty parlor were occupied by women sporting curlers or enough foil to pull in Channel 4 out of the Cities. They were twisting their necks to keep abreast of all the commotion outside, and their stylists were scolding them good-naturedly.

Glokkmann was still exchanging pleasantries with the press below. Grace stepped alongside her to briefly announce the official beginning of the press conference, and then she moved back into the main salon, her remaining papers by her side. I pulled up a chair right behind Glokkmann so I could hear her but no one below could see me. I pretended to take notes as Glokkmann trotted out her tired nonstances, while Grace hovered in a state of agitation. Glokkmann seemed to expect her mind to be read, continuing to talk while regularly reaching an angry hand back and through the partially ajar French doors for water, or a specific document. I wanted to step forward and sneak a hairbrush in there but Grace was vigilant.

At one point, Grace apparently handed Glokkmann the incorrect document, causing the representative to stumble over her facts. It became immediately clear that Glokkmann had no knowledge on the free trade agreement she'd purported to be a huge proponent of. When she couldn't even form a complete sentence on the issue without notes, she began to cough uncontrollably and held out a hand to momentarily excuse herself from the press' view.

She turned on Grace like a striking snake. "What the hell do you think you're doing? Or was this my fault? Did I get my calendar messed up? Was today bring a moron to work day and I forgot?"

I recoiled, and I felt the other occupants of the salon do the same behind me. Grace shrunk into herself and mumbled something.

"What's that?" Glokkmann hissed. "You want to know why I put up with your incompetence? You want to know how I'm going to pull myself out of this mess?"

Grace raised her voice but not her eyes. "I said I'm sorry."

Glokkmann tugged Grace's hair sharply, and Grace shot a surprised glance at her employer. "Yes you are, Grace Swinton, yes you are. Now hand me the correct notes so I can do everyone's favorite circus trick and pull my head out of my own ass."

Trembling, Grace handed Glokkmann a sheet of paper. "I'm really sorry, Sarah."

Glokkmann didn't acknowledge her. She took a deep breath and slapped on an eerily high-energy smile before returning to the balcony. There, she eloquently stated all the reasons she supported free trade. From down below, you wouldn't even be able to see she was reading it word for word.

I was terribly embarrassed for Grace and furious at Glokkmann. I couldn't believe she'd treat an employee like that anywhere, let alone in public. She'd been so angry it was like she didn't even know the rest of us had been here. I was rising to comfort Grace when I heard a loud splat come from the direction of the balcony and wondered if a bird had hit the window. My skin flashed cold. Birds were my nemeses. Have you ever heard the saying that it's good luck to get pooped on by a bird? Me neither. It's also not fun to have them swoop at your head or gawk at you with their beady black eyes. They had the upper hand in this world, no doubt about it, and so I tried exuding fearlessness and a love of all things feathered when I was outdoors. But they knew better.

I began to ease my chair away from the balcony, thinking that if the birds had finally united against me, away from windows would be my best bet. And that's when there was another splat. And then a third. Horrified, I saw that whatever had hit the partially-open French doors leading to the balcony was now oozing a red liquid. The foiled woman in the chair nearest the doors screamed, and Grace yanked the doors open all the way to wrest Sarah Glokkmann to safety. And that's why Glokkmann was in my direct line of sight when one of the bloody blobs met her face and revealed itself to be a soft tomato.

"Woot woot!" I said. Grace shot me a glare before pulling Glokkmann to a chair out of harm's way. Glokkmann snarled that she was fine, and I shot down the stairs three at a time to see who the tomato pitcher was. And when I did, you could have knocked me over with a fly swatter.

SIXTEEN

I RAN NEAR TO where he was standing, holding a bag of tomatoes. Those in the crowd armed with cameras were pointing them at him, snapping or rolling.

"How are you?" He asked when I was within speaking distance. His tone suggested we were old friends meeting for a planned coffee date.

"The pavement get uncomfortable?" I asked Randy Martineau, my parking lot guru. He was wearing the same gray and frayed clothes I'd seen him in the morning after the murder, and his BO hadn't changed either.

He idly studied his bag of tomatoes. "I never stay too long in one place."

"You might want to leave this one," I said. Around me, reporters were clicking away on their handhelds. "I don't know if it's illegal to throw tomatoes at public figures, but it's for sure frowned upon."

"Oh, it's illegal," he said. "Especially if you hit someone. That's why I didn't bring the rest of my crew with me. No one else needs to go to jail. But I never do a crime if I'm unwilling to do the time."

A heavyset reporter for the *St. Paul Pioneer Press* used that opening to jockey in and ask Randy why he'd done the crime.

He methodically brushed his free hand on his pants, leaving a wet trail of tomato residue. "Civil disobedience."

"To what end?" Another reporter asked.

"To get heard. Representative Glokkmann does not represent me. Her opposition to health care is a danger to our democracy, and she's sown so much ill will in the House with her polarizing ignorance that she can no longer meet the obligations of the position to which she was elected."

His accusations echoed Webber's. "How do you know all this?" I asked.

He looked me straight in the eye. "If you look for it, you can find it."

The truth is out there, right? This guy radiated kookiness, but I couldn't shake the feeling of truth in his words, or the sense that he knew something important. "Did you know Bob Webber?"

"Did I know Bob Webber." It didn't come across as a question or a statement. In the background, a police siren blared. We didn't have much time.

"What were you doing in the motel parking lot on Sunday morning?"

"The truth never sleeps. We must be ever-vigilant in our pursuit of it."

"Come on," I said. "Give me something. Who killed Bob Webber?"

But my voice was drowned out by the multitude of questions from the other reporters, who had latched on to the possibility that this man might be connected to the murder they had originally come to town to cover. The crazy drifter espoused his political views and love for anarchy right up until he was handcuffed and shoved into the backseat of a police car. Fortunately, Deputy Wohnt wasn't the arresting officer.

When the police car pulled away, Glokkmann appeared, a smile on her face and her hair more perfect than ever before. She looked like she'd been hit with a beauty brush rather than a tomato. She spoke loud and clear to get everyone's attention. "I've already had my salad. Who wants to join me at the Fortune Café for a main course?"

The reporters laughed at her quick recovery, and I gave her silent points for it. If only she used her powers for good, I thought, tagging along with the throng. She was one twisted sister. As we walked, I wondered if the tomato thrower would be granted visiting privileges in jail. I couldn't tell if he was a crazy agitator or if he genuinely knew something, but I had a stake in finding out. It would be one more thing to ask Kennie tonight.

I wrote myself a note, which was a good thing because as soon as I reached the Fortune Café, all negative thoughts flew from my head like so many dirty bats. My Paul Bunyan breakfast was at least three hours behind me, and I had room for a garlic bagel with a healthy heaping of Greek olive cream cheese and a side of green tea with steamed soy milk added. It was all I could do not to elbow my way to the front of the line. When I got there, Nancy's beautiful smile greeted me. In it was total acceptance, happiness to see me, and a sparkle signaling me she had something funny to share.

"What is it?"

"Don't you mean, 'how have you been?' Haven't seen you in a week! Sid, come on out. Mira's here."

Sid came out from the back, wiping her hands on her flour-dusted apron that proclaimed, "GLBT Is Not a Sandwich." She was something of a baked goods mad scientist and spent a lot of time in the kitchen crafting bagels, scones, and pastries that made you cry they tasted so good, while Nancy ran the front counter and kept everyone happy. It was a perfect arrangement as Sid wasn't what you'd call a people person.

"So I see," she said in my direction. "Did the eggs come in yet?"

Nancy tossed her a loving wink. "I told you I'd bring you the eggs when the shipment arrived."

"But I need the eggs now," Sid said.

I interjected. "I can go on an egg run."

Nancy shook her head. "The truck is due at 1:00. We've got enough eggs until then."

"You sure? I'd be happy to run to the grocery store before I open the library."

Sid softened. "Nancy's probably right. I can make do until 1:00. Nice to see you Mira." She turned to go into the kitchen, but Nancy snuck in a playful pinch on her bottom first. Sid swatted her hand away but I caught her smile.

Nancy returned her attention to me. "You want the usual?"

"Yes. And I also want to know why you had that cat-got-the-mouse grin when I came up to your counter."

"Someone told me that Representative Glokkmann already met her vegetable requirement for the day. It gave me the giggles. Mean-spirited ones, I'll grant you that, but giggles nonetheless."

I glanced over to where Glokkmann was holding court in the packed main room of the Café, a book-lined open space with eclectic tables ringing the edge and lots of natural sunlight and robust green plants. At some point, Tanya Ingebretson had joined the entourage, along with a healthy sprinkling of other locals. It made sense that Glokkmann would want to rub elbows with the most influential people in town. Maybe they even knew each other from their school days. I was pretty sure Tanya was a native of the area.

"It's true," I said. "A protestor caught her square in the face with a tomato. You heard about the dead guy at the motel also?"

Nancy nodded sympathetically. "Murder, people are saying."

"Looks that way."

"You're not involved, right?" Her voice was concerned.

I coughed. I had only yesterday admitted my sleuthing addiction to myself. I wasn't ready to go public with it. "Not directly. Need help making that tea?"

"Don't rush me. I can do two things at once. Speaking of," and her eyes started to twinkle again, "what's this I hear about a tanning and speed dating event at Stub's tonight?"

"I was hoping no one would know about it, and I'd get done early."

"So you *are* helping! I thought Kennie was joking."

"I was tricked."

Nancy reached into the glass display case to grab the biggest, freshest-looking bagel this side of New York City. "You might find love there."

I wagged my head vigorously. "I'm into self-love now."

"That'll make you go blind."

"Ha ha. No, I'm strictly working at this event. Don't suppose you and Sid want to come lend a gal a hand?"

"Sorry," she said, slathering olive-laced cream cheese onto the bagel before wrapping it in wax paper. "Tuesday night is TV night for us. Popcorn and root beer in front of the boob tube." She bobbed her head toward the crowd in the main room. "You just here for lunch or are you covering Glokkmann for the paper?"

"Funny you should ask. I might be doing a little article on her."

She finished filling a mug with hot water, popped in an unbleached bag of tea leaves, and set it on a tray next to my bagel. "Ron ask for it?"

Dang she knew me well. "Does he ever know what he wants? I better get to it." I paid for my purchase, grabbed the bagel in one hand and the tea in the other, and sauntered to the outskirts of the room. I was glad I hadn't sat in the center because Tanya had chosen that moment to lead the assembled reporters in a "nondenominational prayer that gives thanks to God." I bowed my head so anyone cheating on the prayer wouldn't see me chewing.

After the lengthy prayer, neither Tanya nor Glokkmann ate. Instead, Tanya played the role of "voter" and interviewed Glokkmann about what she called "family values issues." They set it up like a fireside chat, two friends talking, with a dozen reporters scribbling down notes. Tanya mostly lobbed softballs: "How important are schools to you?" "How crucial do you think a strong family base is for our community?" I tuned it out and scarfed my lunch, wondering if anyone could hear me moan. The combination of chewy bagel and creamy cool cheese accented with salty bits of green and black olives was embarrassingly good.

Unfortunately, the clock was running out for me. I was hoping to meet with Glokkmann one-on-one to ask some questions, but it was looking like I wouldn't have time for that before work. I was about to give it up for the day and head out when Tanya's question fried my ears.

"What are your views on gay marriage?" She had the prim smile of a nanny changing a smelly diaper.

Glokkmann, the consummate politician, responded. "I think they are welcome to their personal lifestyle choices, but marriage is sacrosanct and should remain between a man and a woman."

They were talking about people who were gay like they were some weird hybrid zoo creature. Tanya nodded approvingly and said, "Shall we say a prayer for lesbians?"

Grace stepped over and whispered something about gay men in Tanya's ear. She listened, and then frowned. "Oh no, dear, they can't be helped. Just the lesbians."

My last bite of bagel caught in my throat. I was reaching for a book off the shelf to lob at Tanya's superior smile when I saw Curtis Poling stand in the back of the room. I'd been so fixated on my bagel and Glokkmann that I hadn't noticed he was here. Curtis was the Senior Sunset stud, a 90-year-old man with beautiful clear eyes and teeth that were as perfect as the day he'd bought them. Many in town thought he was crazy, probably because he could be found fishing off the roof of the Sunset on any given day. Those of us who knew him personally knew that was just a quirk that kept him from getting bored. He was still as smart as a steel trap, probably too smart for his own good. I wondered how he'd snuck out of the Sunset this day. "Phoo-ey," he said.

I spotted a few other locals around him nodding their heads. Tanya ignored him and went on with her prayer.

"I said *phoo*-ey," Curtis said. "Tanya Ingebretson, you've been mean-spirited since you were a little girl, and that's just about enough. That's not how your parents raised you."

Tanya flushed. "The Bible says—"

"Bible shmible. You're a bully, always have been. Just because you're hanging out with a whole bunch of other bullies on that issue doesn't make you any less wrong."

"Shut up, Curtis Poling! I walk in The Light!"

"Looks like the Dark Ages from where I'm sitting," someone behind Curtis muttered loudly. I craned my neck and saw it was the owner of the new flower shop. I wanted to hug him. His comment set off a firestorm of others, and suddenly reporter and local alike were distancing themselves from Tanya's words. Even Glokkmann looked like she wished she could beam herself to a different conversation.

I became aware that Nancy and Sid were standing behind me. I turned and offered a half-smile. Nancy's face was a mix of sad and grateful. Sid had smoke coming out of her ears.

"If only Tanya knew how close she was to the enemy," I whispered.

Sid shrugged. "She knows. What she doesn't know is that I sneezed in her food. She should be fully gay by the next full moon. Her husband will surely be relieved."

"Sid!" Nancy gasped and swatted her arm. "You wouldn't dare sneeze in someone's food."

Sid and I exchanged a grin and returned our attention to the main room. Curtis was on his way out in protest, and most of the townspeople were following him. Glokkmann stood to pretend that she was calling the press conference to an end rather than acknowledge that it imploded. She ignored Tanya, and I couldn't but hope that Tanya would get to feel the sharp side of the representative's tongue later.

I was about to leave on that positive note when Glokkmann called my name.

"Mira!"

I turned. How did she know who I was? But of course—Grace was standing behind her. I walked over and held out my hand. Up close, she looked older than I expected, or more tired. Her makeup was cracking at the edges. "Pleased to meet you, Representative Glokkmann. Quite a gathering."

"Call me Sarah," she said. "Grace tells me you're a reporter here in town, and you want to do a story on my work here?"

Not what I'd call work, but I wasn't writing what anyone would call a story, so I didn't split hairs. "I would. I'll of course cover today's talking points, but I'd also like to ask you some questions. I have to go open the library now, but maybe tomorrow?"

"I'm sure we can figure something out. Grace, how does my schedule look?"

Grace consulted her handheld. "Your next opening is Thursday."

"You plan on staying that long?" I asked.

Her tense smile tightened. "I feel it's my responsibility to listen to my constituents when Congress isn't in session. I'll be in Battle Lake as long as that takes."

Or for the murder investigation to wrap up. "Great! What time Thursday, and where would you like to meet?"

"How about 10:00 a.m. at the library?"

"Perfect," I said. "We don't open until noon so that would give us uninterrupted time to talk. I appreciate it."

"It would be helpful if the library was open earlier," she said, her brow furrowing.

"I agree. Our funding was cut."

"Oh no, that's not right. That's not right at all. I will have to see what I can do about that. In the meanwhile, what do you say about changing the Thursday library hours?"

"Changing them to what?"

"Ten to whatever time you're scheduled to close."

"I can do that this Thursday, but like I said, there's no funding for longer hours."

She wrinkled her nose. "There must be a way to cut corners. You like your job?"

I didn't like the direction this conversation was taking. Yet. "Yeah, I do."

"And does the town love its library?"

"I think so."

"Then you'll find a way, I know you will, even if it means taking a pay cut. In tough times, we all have to tighten our belts." She nodded her head brusquely. "I'll see you Thursday at 10:00 a.m."

"Thank you so much," I said acidly. Out of the corner of my eye, I noted Tanya eavesdropping on our conversation and smiling broadly. I mentally stuck my tongue out at her.

"My pleasure," Glokkmann said, but she was already looking over my shoulder. Most of the reporters had left.

On my way out, I heard Glokkmann thanking Nancy for her wonderful food and hospitality. I wondered if Sid was going to let the representative walk out without giving her a piece of her mind.

I left all that behind me to run the library for the next six hours at what were already poverty wages. I certainly could volunteer to work to keep the library open longer hours, but that wouldn't solve the problem of slashed funding for basic community services—schools, medical care, libraries. I fumed for hours about how that woman had made me feel guilty for doing my job, but at the end of the day, I had bigger fish to fry.

Or backs to spray. I still wasn't a hundred percent clear on how Kennie had tricked me into tonight's gig. Really, it was Mrs. Berns' fault because I wouldn't be indebted to Kennie if not for her. I was rolling that negative thought around in my head, getting ready to close up the library, when in walked Conrad, marching like he was on full parade. He pounded toward where I stood behind the front counter and held out his hand. Feeling peevish, I didn't take it.

"What can I do for you, Mr. Berns?"

"It's what you can do for my mother. Allow me to speak plainly. She's going to be moved to a nursing home where I can guarantee she's safe, and I need your help in making a smooth transition for her."

I swung from one angry tree to another. "Safe? What kind of life is 'safe'?"

He pounded his fist on the countertop, and I jumped. "For God sakes, you've seen her in the hospital! She almost died on Sunday. Do you want that on your shoulders?"

I sucked in an angry breath. "I might not always agree with her decisions. You might not always agree with her decisions. But she's earned the right to make her own choices and to live with the consequences."

He leaned in closely, his nose advancing toward me like a paring knife. "I know she cares about you. If you care about her, you'll encourage her to move to the new nursing home, and you'll tell my sister that you think it's for the best. I don't know why, but Elizabeth has come to respect your input."

I didn't back down. "Do you even know your mother? Have you even asked any of her friends what she's like, or do you just come in and tell everyone how it's going to be? Because if you asked around, you'd find that your mom is pretty well-respected in this community, and she's happy. And she's settling down." I had a hard time following the script but soldiered on. "She's engaged to an employed man and she's meeting with a life coach. She's turning her life around."

He ran his hand over his face, and for a moment, I saw the man behind the curtain. "I want her out of harm's way. That's all. I just want my mother to be protected, and to live a life that would make my dad proud."

"What about a life that would make her proud?"

He didn't answer, instead turning a neat 180 on his back heel and marching out the way he'd come.

He left me agitated by thoughts of Mrs. Berns being forcibly led away despite her best attempts to get her granny on, and this agitation slowed me down. I got out of work later than expected. I had only enough time to run home and check on Tiger Pop and Luna, who were both sunning themselves in the backyard, before I cruised back into town and parked behind Stub's. I was dismayed to see the lot was already filling up. Kennie was equally disappointed when I walked in, but for different reasons.

"Sugar pie, I thought we agreed you'd come early to help decorate the tables and storm up some conversation starters?"

I had no patience for her whining. "It's been a crappy day. You're lucky I'm here at all. But since I am, how's this for conversational springboards for tonight's festivities: 'Why are you orange?' or 'Can you believe we paid for this?'"

"Now now, that's no attitude. This is a fun night! You're a sparkly hostess! Come with me." She dragged me over to the spray tan booth she'd set up. It consisted of four cloth room dividers arranged so they formed a portable room in a roughly square shape. A curtain lay draped over the single opening so people could walk in and out without moving the dividers. Inside the makeshift room rested a single chair, which Kennie informed me was for the shirts of the tanners, and a bench which contained the MagiTan® spraying equipment, hair cover-ups, and white paper towels for the clients to tuck into the waist of their pants so no orange smeared on them. My instructions were to only spray faces and upper bodies.

I listened to half of what she said, wondering if I was supposed to have some sort of license. Any job that entailed changing the color of someone's skin should require formal training and a standardized certification. "I'm only doing this because I told you I would, you know," I said pettily. "I already found out that Swydecker doesn't have an alibi for the night of the murder."

She raised an eyebrow. "Then you certainly won't want to hear that he was with a woman that night."

"What?" I thought back to my conversation with him. He'd been the picture of resigned honesty. "He said he wasn't with anyone the night of the murder. Why would he lie if he had someone to corroborate his whereabouts and get him off the hook?"

She tapped her long red fingernail against her chin and pretended to ponder that idea. "Let's see. Why would a married man running for political office hide the fact that he'd spent the night with a woman?"

I pictured his empty wedding ring finger. "The woman wasn't his wife."

"Bingo! But don't be too disappointed. I have even more interesting information to share. We've found enough evidence at the scene of the crime to name a suspect."

My ears perked. "Not Swydecker, right?"

"You'll have to wait until after your shift to find out. When some of those men take off their shirts and you have to push aside back hair to get to their skin, you might lose your resolve without incentive to stay."

Or my lunch. I looked longingly at the rows of glittering glass bottles behind the bar, slapped myself, and walked, head down, into the booth just as the line began to form outside it.

The only way I could get through the hour of spraying the bodies of strangers was by pretending I was a prison guard delousing them, and that they were all going away for a very long time. The patrons' reactions ran the gamut from shy to sheepish to excited. Mostly, though, they were nervous and trying to hide it. The only person who acknowledged the strangeness of the evening was a sweet woman in her late twenties with a slight limp. I'd seen her around town and thought she worked at one of the gift shops. She was constantly in the library checking out books on animals, but she was painfully shy and I didn't know her name.

When her back was turned, she said, "How long have you been doing this?"

"About thirty minutes."

She laughed politely. "No, not tonight. I meant in your life."

"Yup," I said.

"Oh." She held out her arms when I asked. "This is kinda weird, then."

"I'm sorry."

She coughed and reached for the bra she'd set over the back of the chair and then caught herself, squaring her shoulders and holding her arms out again. "I'm not going to meet anyone if I don't step out of my comfort zone, am I?"

My sympathy for her squelched my sarcastic urges. "It could be a fun night."

"Yes," she said firmly. "Will the spray cover up my tattoo?"

I glanced at the lower back art, the head of a German Shepherd above the name "Toby." According to the dates, he had died last year.

"I don't think so, and it's only temporary in any case. Do you still want the spray?"

"Sure," she said. "I've seen you working at the library. Is this your new part-time job?"

"Not if I can help it. Was Toby your dog?"

"Yes."

"I'm sorry. I live with a part German shepherd. Her name is Luna. I know how easy it is to love your dogs." I finished spraying her back and instructed her to face me. She was kind enough to cover her breasts with her hands. The spray lines would be odd, but it made us both much more comfortable.

"Yes. It is."

Her shoulders were quavering a little, so I finished quickly. "Good luck tonight."

She thanked me, got dressed, and left. I returned to the drudgery of coating people who were too embarrassed to talk, which was fine by me. I was doing great until the very last gentleman entered my booth, his coupon in hand. He was in his early thirties and thin, sporting a long Ichabod Crane neck with a bobbing Adam's apple. I gave him the spiel.

"We'll treat this just like a tanning booth. First, take your shirt off." He complied. "And your glasses." He slid them off his nose and set them on his neatly folded shirt. "Hold your arms out like you're a scarecrow." I sprayed his front. We were doing great until my sprayer clogged.

"Excuse me," I said. "I have to go rinse this. I'll be right back." A quick rinse under hot water, and I had the sprayer working again in under two minutes. The end was in sight, and so by the time I returned to the tanning room, I was almost in a good mood. Until I pulled back the curtain on the tanning room and saw Ichabod standing there, facing me and completely naked. I squeaked, and then, I swear I couldn't help it, my eyes shot to his down-below before zipping back up to his face. My cheeks burned. Never underestimate the skinny guys was the hard-earned lesson there.

I covered embarrassment with indignation. "What the put-your-pants-on is going on here?"

He might have blushed, but it was impossible to tell because before leaving I had sprayed his face the color of a tropical sunset. "You told me to treat this like a tanning booth. I tan naked at the tanning booth. Tan lines, you know. Everybody tans naked," he added, as if I hadn't gotten the memo. He looked ready to cry, but defiant, like he didn't want to admit that this mortifying situation was all his fault.

He looked so, well, naked. I felt bad for him. I sucked in a deep breath. "You're right that I did say to treat this like a tanning booth. I'm sorry I wasn't clearer. I really should have been." I indicated his lower torso without looking directly at it. Okay, I might have snuck in one more glance. Goodness. "This is only top-up tanning. Nothing from the waist down. I'll step out so you can get dressed."

"But what about my back?" He whined. "Will you still tan my back?"

"As soon as your pants are back on." I stepped out and inhaled deeply. I was certain I was going to have nightmares about anteaters tonight.

He called me back in once he was dressed, and we both made a Herculean effort to avoid eye contact. He made awkward conversational attempts, but accidental nudity is hard to recover from. I quickly spritzed his back and exited the booth to help Kennie herd the lovelorn singles to their grazing ground.

While I'd been spraying the two dozen odd clients, she'd been plying them with liquor. As a result, almost everyone in Stub's back room was approximately the color of traffic cones, and blitzed. They were voluntarily sex-segregated, the women on one side of the room giggling and staring at the men, and the men on the other shoving their hands in their pockets and dearly wishing the guy next to them would morph into a TV. It was like being at a Martian dentists' convention: a bunch of boring, drunk, orange creatures standing around uncomfortably.

Kennie had deliberately kept the male/female ratio as close to even as possible. She'd told me the plan for the night was to seat one man at each table, and then she would blow a whistle. Each woman would charge toward the table she wanted and then have five minutes to talk up the man sitting there. When the next whistle blew, the women would stand and move one table to their right. I calculated it should take less than an hour to get through this skin auction, I'd get the dirt on the suspect from Kennie, and I'd be home to wash my eyes with hydrogen peroxide before 10:00 pm.

Kennie explained the rules to the participants, and I helped her seat one man per table. Then we stepped out of the way.

The fast-action love tango was surprisingly painful to watch, hopeful singles striving to flirt, make small talk, and open their heart in the space of five minutes. It was like watching an excruciating, high-speed job interview play itself out over and over again. The worst was when one person at a table showed an immediate interest and the other person did not, which I observed was frequently the case with Ichabod Crane, my pee-peeper. It got so by the end of the night, I was feeling even sorrier for him than before. I overheard him trotting out the same jokes to woman after woman, and they weren't buying it:

"Hey, I'm Darcy," he'd say, "and I just want to know, if airports are so safe, why do they call them terminals?"

If the woman laughed politely, he'd follow that with, "and have you ever noticed that how long a minute is depends on what side of the bathroom door you're on?" That one was almost a guarantee that the woman would excuse herself to get a drink, but if she was kind enough to stay put, he'd roll out his ace in the hole. "There seems to be something wrong with my cell phone." And he'd pop it out and flip it open. Yes, flip it open. "It doesn't have your number in it."

I finally couldn't stand it any longer. I slipped in the seat across from him at the next whistle. He was by now so dejected from the process that he didn't look up, just said in a morose voice, "Hey, I'm Darcy, and I just want to know, if airports are so—"

"Stop it."

He glanced up. "What are you doing here? Are you a speed dater too?" He returned his gaze to his lap, embarrassed. "I'm sorry, but you're not really my type."

"What?" I was insulted before I realized I didn't care. "Never mind. You're not my type either. But you might meet a nice woman if you stop being so pitiful."

"I don't know what you mean," he said pitifully.

"Look, despite the fact that you depantsed yourself, you seem like a nice guy. Am I right?"

"My mother thinks so."

"Jeez. See what I mean? You talk too much. You're on automatic spiel, and you're not even listening to the women across from you. Everyone likes to be listened to."

He pulled out a well-worn book from his back pocket. "Not according to *Manly Man: The Guide to Irresistibility*. Women like their men funny and forceful."

I chucked the book across the room and saw two men scoop it up quick like seagulls on a hot dog. "There's no prescription for love. You have to be yourself if you want to find someone who loves you." Who did I think I was? Me dispensing dating advice was like Humpty Dumpty telling people how to sit.

"But no one likes me when I'm myself," he said in a tiny voice.

"Try me. We have forty-five seconds left."

"I'm feeling kind of insecure right now. Could I have a hug?"

"Try harder."

He drew in a shaky breath. "Hi. My name is Darcy. I'm an online game developer. I make around $40,000 a year and hide most of it in a Crisco can under the sink because I'm afraid of banks. If I was an animal, I'd be a fish that no one has ever discovered. I've only kissed one female besides my mom, and we got our braces tangled and had to be brought to the E.R. to separate them. She never wanted to see me again, which was hard because we were in the same homeroom."

I held up my hand. I couldn't take it anymore. "Do you have anything positive to say at all?"

He dragged his eyes to meet mine with great effort. "I volunteer at the Humane Society, and I love it. It's the only place I'm happy. I spend every free moment helping out."

My light bulb went off, though it was dim. "Hold it right there." I looked around for the woman with Toby tattooed on her back but couldn't find her anywhere. As a last ditch effort, I searched the bathroom and came across her hiding in a corner, clutching a drink like it was a life preserver. "You okay?" I asked.

She had tear streaks on her carrot-colored face and wiped them away quickly. "I don't think this is for me."

"Care to give it one more chance?"

She shook her head. "I think I want to go home."

"Please? It can't get much worse, right?"

She smiled tiredly and slammed what was left of her drink. "If it'll make you feel better. I suppose you get in trouble if we're not all at the tables like we're supposed to be."

"Sure." I led her over to Darcy. They might not find love, but I had a good feeling they'd be nice to each other. "Darcy, this is ...?"

"Cindy," she said, averting her eyes.

"And Cindy, this is Darcy." I pushed her in the chair.

"Hi, Cindy. My name is Darcy." He still looked demoralized. "Why, if airplanes are so safe, do they call them terminals?"

I launched evil eye daggers at him—had he not listened to one word I'd said?—but stopped when I heard a faint snort-hiccup and realized Cindy was laughing. Darcy, encouraged, shared his second and third joke and moved on to a fourth, and by the time I realized I wasn't needed, Cindy was laughing so hard she was doubled over and Darcy was staring at her with a dazed, goofy grin.

The world is a strange place, and I'd had enough of it for the night. I tracked down Kennie, who'd pulled the beefiest guy out of the line-up and was trying to convince him, between whistle blasts, that he'd need to come by her place to fill out more paperwork. I stepped between them, and he took the opportunity to dash away.

"Honey! I was making a love connection."

"He looked scared."

"Humph. What do you want?"

"I've had enough. I'm going home. Tell me what you know."

"But the night isn't done yet! There's still four more rotations to go."

I scanned the room. "Have you looked around? You put too many candles on each table, and it's melting the color right off their faces. Anyone who hasn't left in shame is either paired up already or not gonna be. It's time to call it a night."

She put her hands on her hips. "Fine, but do you have to turn everything into a negative?"

"Sorry," I said through gritted teeth. "I'm *positive* I never want to do this again."

To my surprise, she laughed. "You're a piece of work, Mira James. And for that, I'll give you a twofer. The first one: you know the drifter who pelted Sarah with tomatoes today?"

"Yeah, I was there. He's got a good arm."

"And I think he deserves a medal, but that's beside the point. He was released today because Sarah didn't want to press charges as long as he left Battle Lake immediately. He was driven to the county line this afternoon."

"What is this, *Gunsmoke*?"

She ignored me. "As to the murder investigation, like I was saying earlier, evidence has been recovered from the scene. A couple medium, light brown hairs were found in Webber's fist and a faint but muddy shoe print that doesn't belong to him was also discovered."

My throat swelled until I remembered that my shoes hadn't been muddy. Or had they? "Light brown and not dark brown?"

Kennie studied me. "Definitely not dark brown."

"Sarah Glokkmann has medium length, light brown hair."

"I know!" Kennie clapped her hands in glee.

"So, the police know whose hairs and footprint they are?"

"They have a couple guesses. How fast this moves depends on whether those people willingly give up DNA samples."

"You'll tell me when you find out?"

"We'll see."

I knew that was all I was going to get from her, and it was more than I'd expected. "You know, Kennie, you're not all bad."

She winked. "Just bad enough."

We said our goodbyes and I was about to write this night off as "not as atrocious as it could have been" when I ran smack dab into Deputy Gary Wohnt.

SEVENTEEN

"You're too late for the speed dating, I'm afraid. You'll have to catch it next round." My heart was whining like a puppy.

"Kennie Rogers still here?" He growled.

I pointed behind me to where Kennie was dancing seductively and alone to Def Leppard's "Pour Some Sugar on Me." She didn't appear to have any takers.

He nodded his acknowledgment. And he still wore the mirrored shades.

"You ever wonder what the world looks like without those glasses on?" I asked.

And immediately regretted my smart aleck words as he slid the sunglasses off and pinned me to the wall with his black and bottomless eyes. I tried not to let on that my knees had gone wobbly, but it was hard. If he was a superhero, Gary Wohnt would be the Black-eyed Truthinator. "I stole Twinkies from John Fuch's lunch box in first grade, but only because my mom wouldn't buy me any and I've never stolen anything since."

Did his eyes twinkle, or were they merely catching the reflection of the disco ball swirling at the center of the room? "You give any more thought to your whereabouts the night of the murder, or more specifically, the morning the cleaning woman discovered the body of Bob Webber?"

I steeled myself. I was a champion liar. I could keep a secret better than the ocean. But what was it about those eyes that delved into my soul? I exhaled noisily. Might as well face the music now, when I had a façade of control over the outcome. "Look, I was at the motel that night. I heard the maid scream the next morning, and I ran in to see if she needed help. She had called 911, confirmed that Webber was dead, and told me there was nothing for me to do. I didn't touch anything. Lord knows I don't need to be found next to any more dead bodies, so I left."

"Is that all?"

I knew he wanted me to finger Mrs. Berns and her boy toy, but I wouldn't do it. My personal resolve may be periodically weak, but when it came to protecting my friends, I was Fort Knox. I tried throwing him off the trail. "I slept with Johnny Leeson the night before, if that's what you want to know."

He blinked rapidly for a moment, but it was enough to break the laser spell of his gaze. "I know."

"Then you know what I know. Is there anything else?"

"I'll be in touch," he said gruffly, sliding his glasses back on as he walked toward Kennie, who was now illustrating to the dwindling audience her take on the quickest way to bring Sexy Back.

I drew a deep breath and scurried out while the scurrying was good.

I woke the next morning finally beginning to feel normal again. I'd gotten sufficient sleep two nights in a row, and my stomach was back in the game. I spent some quality downtime with my plants and animals before cruising to Alexandria to pick up Mrs. Berns. She was so anxious to escape the hospital that she was waiting curbside in a wheelchair when I arrived.

"I told you I'd be here by 10 o'clock."

"Pah. I knew you'd be early. Help me get on these sticks and load up my bags." She had a pair of old-fashioned wooden crutches strapped to the back of the wheelchair and a suitcase next to her.

"Wouldn't a wheelchair be more manageable?"

"I'd sooner have a colostomy bag," she said. "People see you in a wheelchair, they think you're weak. They take advantage of you."

I unstrapped them and held them out to her. She looked bruised and tiny in the wheelchair, but her eyes were as fiery as ever. "And on crutches?"

Almost before my sentence was out of my mouth, she'd snatched a crutch out of my hand and swung it in a whipsnake arch. I ducked to avoid getting whacked.

"Point taken," I said. I eased her into the car where she stayed while I made a quick run to Freda's room for my promised visit. I made sure she had what she needed and gave her my word that I'd be back again soon.

The drive back to Battle Lake was pleasant, a last explosion of red, gold, and orange before the white fist of winter clamped down on the landscape. The air smelled like change, the turn of the wheel that leads to dormancy, cold, and rest. But we weren't there yet. Today was about unseasonable warmth, the scent of brown leaves cooking in the sun, and maple trees so brightly colored that they sang. While I navigated the road, I filled Mrs. Berns in on what I'd learned, minus any mention of her fiancé's bad behavior or her son visiting me at the library. I didn't want to cause her unnecessary stress. We both agreed that the hairs found in the room were a good sign unless Glenn Vanderbrick or any of his guests also had long, sandy-brown hair. I assumed the police had already ruled that out, which is why they considered the hairs and the shoe print to be real evidence. We also agreed that it wasn't such a good time to be Sarah Glokkmann or Arnold Swydecker.

"All politicians are the same," Mrs. Berns said. "Just door-to-door salesmen with a wider audience. Don't trust a one of them."

"I dunno. Swydecker seemed different."

"You mean different from the other unfaithful husbands you've known?"

"I'm not a fan of his alleged personal choices. I'm talking about his politics. He really seemed sincere and dedicated."

"I bet he did. Say, I've got a bridge I'd like to sell you. It crosses from West Battle Lake to the Mississippi, and underneath lives a magical troll who poops diamonds and blueberries. Good deal, going fast."

I changed the subject. "Your fiancé meeting you at the Sunset?"

"If he knows what's good for him."

I still didn't know how I'd broach the subject of Bernard's checkered past, but I was formulating a plan that might involve a hint of blackmail. "I've been thinking that it would be a good idea for me to interview him."

"What for?" She asked. She was studying me suspiciously.

"To completely rule him out as a suspect. And to find out why he didn't like Bob Webber."

"Seems your goals are in opposition to each other."

I'd been thinking the same thing. "Knowledge is power."

"Knowledge is shit compared to a Taser when it comes to power. I dare you to think your way out of an electrical volt designed to make you cry out your feet."

"Nevertheless," I said, trying to get her back on topic. "Do you think I could have some time with Bernard? We don't know a lot about him, you know."

She beetled her brows. If she did in fact know about his past, a possibility I'd entertained, she wasn't letting on. "Bernard and I are going out for a fancy dinner tonight to celebrate my homecoming. Why don't you join us?"

That was too easy. "The catch?"

"His name is Johnny Leeson."

My face grew hot, and she chortled. "I don't know if that's shame or anticipation on your face, girlie. Knowing you, probably both."

"Our night at the motel didn't go as well as planned."

"Really? Did you know that cows have four legs? Because that's another unexpected bit of information I like people to know."

"It's even worse than you think. I threw up." I shuddered as I re-lived the scene. "He saw it. He held my hair."

She whistled. "Were you naked or in clothes?"

"In clothes!" I said indignantly.

"Thank God for small favors. Nothing less attractive than a naked girl throwing up. There's no recovery from that."

"You think I can recover from this?"

"You want to?"

"I don't know," I said honestly.

"Christ, I don't care. I just love to watch you make a fool of yourself. So I called Johnny this morning to say you were having dinner with me and Bernard tonight and you wanted him to join us. And if you want to talk to Bernard, you'll have to show."

"But I'm only talking to Bernard to help you!"

"That'll teach you to trust an old lady. Now pull up in the handicapped spot right there. If these crutches don't buy me better parking, then I'm going back to the wheelchair."

EIGHTEEN

I'D WORKED AT LOOKING pretty the night Johnny had invited me to the motel room, and look where that'd gotten me. Lip gloss, mascara, and shaved legs equal face over toilet, eternal shame, and a dead body. I wasn't going to make that mistake twice. I loped on over to Stella's straight from my library shift, not even bothering to brush my hair.

"You look beautiful."

"Huhn?" I swiveled in the narrow entryway. I hadn't seen Johnny approach.

"How are you feeling?" He looked concerned, handsome, emotionally vulnerable.

I cleared my throat. "Better." I told myself not to meet his eyes, not to look up into those hypnotizing blue seapools, but I couldn't help it. We locked gazes and the charge was electric. "Actually, I feel like the biggest loser in town. I can't believe you saw me throw up."

He smiled and grabbed my hand. I wanted to pull away, but didn't. "Don't worry about it."

"Some of it came out my nose."

The corner of his mouth quirked up. He didn't disagree.

"I've decided we're a doomed relationship and sworn off men forever. Well, at least non-fiberglass ones."

He squeezed my hand and scanned the restaurant for Mrs. Berns. "Give me a chance."

"I did."

"Give me another one."

I was saved from a response by the sound of Mrs. Berns' yell. "Over here, lovebirds!"

The whole restaurant turned. I tried to slide my hand out of Johnny's, but he wouldn't let me. He walked confidently to the table, dragging me behind like toilet paper on his shoe.

"How're you feeling, Mrs. Berns?"

"Not as fine as you look, Johnny Leeson." She was right. The man wore blue jeans like a spoon wore honey, and I could see the cut of his sculpted shoulders through his shirt. "Have you met my fiancé, Mr. Bernard Mink?"

Johnny held out his hand. "Pleased to meet you, sir."

Bernard shook it but didn't acknowledge me. I wondered if Mrs. Berns had told him I wanted to talk. Actually, studying them side by side, I realized they weren't a bad-looking couple. With their mouths closed, you might be tricked into believing they were your average retired pair setting off into the sunset in their RV. That is, if you could overlook the nasty bruises turning green on their faces and the cast on Mrs. Berns' leg. Bernard was considerably younger than his date, but no spring chicken. He wore a nice polo shirt over a pair of khakis. Mrs. Berns had slipped on elastic-waisted pants and a pink and lime green blouse accented by plastic old-lady jewelry. The only good thing about a wedding between her and Bernard is that afterward, she could go back to dressing with the pizzazz she was known for. But I wasn't going to let it get that far.

Johnny pulled out my chair and asked if I'd like something to drink.

"Water's fine," I said. The restaurant had a simple and welcoming cabin-and-fresh-flowers décor, and a faint jazz tune encouraged conversation without overwhelming it.

"As I was saying," Bernard said to Mrs. Berns, resuming their conversation, "for all intensive purposes, the sooner the wedding, the better."

"For all intents and purposes," I said.

"Exactly," he said.

It was too much. "You two are trying to get married sooner than Halloween? That's not even two weeks away." I gave Mrs. Berns warning eyes. Forget avoiding stressing her, or even me wanting to get her back in her sassy clothes. I'd rather have her dress like a granny into infinity than bind herself to this loser any sooner than necessary. I'd have to hurry my plan, but my hands were tied until I could get Bernard alone.

"You *can* hurry love," Bernard said. "I want to make her my woman for all modernity."

I considered asking him to retarditerate his point, but I couldn't stand to hear him butcher the language any more. I changed the subject. "How's your online class going, Mrs. Berns?"

Not my smartest move. She filled us in with such hyper-specific detail that we were all too embarrassed to look at each other by the time our food came. We ate with our heads down, shoveling the food in quickly to get the night over with. Mrs. Berns won the clean plate award, clearing her filet mignon and baked potato before it got cold.

"Damn that's better than hospital food." She pushed her plate away, a wide smile on her plate. "Bernard, I believe it's time for a kiss."

"But I'm not done with my steak yet," he groused.

She flicked him on the forehead like a bad dog and then pulled him in close. If you've ever watched old people kiss, you've noticed that they appear to have to pop through a small, invisible barrier to touch lips, like two opposite pole magnets shoved together. Mrs. Berns did not kiss like that. Her magnet was always turned the right way, and her public passion made me even more uncomfortable than her tales of studying human sexuality. Johnny tapped my leg, and I realized I'd been staring.

"I'm full. Want to move over to the bar so we can give these two some privacy?"

I looked longingly at my half-eaten brick oven margherita pizza. It was delicious.

"I'll have them box it up for you," Mrs. Berns said out of the corner of her mouth. I was unsurprised to learn that she had 360-degree vision while kissing. She was a modern miracle when it came to the art of love.

"Thanks," I said, but made no move to stand.

"And Bernard will talk to you before you leave."

That's what I needed to hear. "We'll be at the bar." I crammed my hands into my pockets so Johnny couldn't grab one of them again and followed him into the other room. It was packed, even on a Wednesday, but he found a quiet corner. We nursed our water, standing in uncomfortable silence.

"Mira?" He asked. "Do you like me?"

Ohmygodyes. Liked him so much that I didn't want to jinx him, that I'd rather move to India than ruin his life with my bad luck, that I wanted to throw him to the ground right now and ride him like a merry-go-round. "Yeah."

"Then why does it always feel like you're running away?" He took my hand again. I squelched the urge to not yank it back.

"I'm a little damaged," I said, embarrassed that I'd blushed when I said it. "I'm not ... your type."

He pulled me in close. I was about to make some crack about us taking notes from Mrs. Berns and Bernard when his warm lips brushed against mine, soft, and then harder, his tongue gently exploring the edges of my mouth. I sighed and fell against his hard body, loving the feel of his hand in my hair. He pulled back slightly and moved his mouth to my ear, landing soft butterfly kisses on the edge. "That's for me to decide," he whispered huskily.

"Yes," I said, not sure what I was agreeing to.

"Will you go to Mrs. Berns' wedding with me?"

At that moment, I would have gone to the landfill to pick out furniture with him. "Uh-hunh." I pushed back against his mouth. His tongue was magic. I heard a soft chuckle, a vibration against my ear, before his mouth moved to the base of my neck. I swear the only reason I didn't mount him like a farm animal right there in the bar was that a siren blared past the front of Stella's, an ambulance followed by two police cars. My heart clutched. They were racing toward the north side of the town, and there were lots of people I cared about on the north side of town.

I stepped back, tamping down my libido with fear. "I have to see what's happening."

His eyes were stormy with passion but cleared quickly. "I'll drive."

We raced outside and realized it would be quicker to walk than drive. Stella's was on a rise on Lake Street, and we could see that the emergency vehicles had screamed past us and pulled into the Big Chief Motor Lodge a half mile directly north. It was their second time there in under a week. We dashed north, covering the distance in less than five minutes, arriving out of breath and in time to witness the ambulance crew hurrying up to the lakeside second story with a stretcher between them.

It was such an odd juxtaposition of the scene after Webber was found that I felt unbalanced in the cool October air and reached out to Johnny. He grabbed my arm to steady me and we kept moving forward, on the scene in time to see the ambulance crew hurry down the stairs and toward us with an unconscious Arnold Swydecker on a gurney, skin gray, yellow foam bubbling out the corner of his mouth.

NINETEEN

GRACE SWINTON FOLLOWED CLOSELY behind, her eyes wide with shock. Gary Wohnt tried to detain her, but she pushed him away, yelling meaningless, angry words. He calmed her down, restraining her by holding her upper arms and speaking to her calmly. I was close enough to hear him tell her he'd drive her to the hospital, and her wailing in pain. She was acting a lot like a woman who was seeing a loved one carted away in an ambulance.

The realization set me on my heels. Swinton was in love with Swydecker. I tried to fit that epiphany into the puzzle of Webber's murder but didn't know where it belonged. Was she Swydecker's alibi, the woman he'd rather go to jail for than reveal as his lover? The only thing certain was that being involved with her boss' opponent must have caused her a great deal of stress. Enough stress to kill, though?

Bernard showed up on our heels, having left the gimpy Mrs. Berns on the street out front of Stella's. After some begging, I convinced Johnny that it was absolutely necessary to go back and drive Mrs. Berns home because she shouldn't be so active this soon after her accident.

Bernard insisted on staying to dig around for a story, which struck me as incredibly tacky, but I wasn't sure I was any better.

The ambulance pulled out, as did Wohnt with Swinton in his car. I didn't recognize the police officer who had stayed behind to secure the scene, but he was determined that Bernard and I were not to interfere, were not even to have access to the second floor. Bernard listened before charging to the lobby to make a call on his cell phone, presumably to his editor. I did not listen, which is why when the officer strode to his car to retrieve his police tape, I was able to sprint to the second floor unnoticed.

Swydecker's door was open and I darted in. I knew I had only a few seconds. A quick visual scan showed me the exact same room I'd been in during the interview except for a messy pile of paper pooling on the floor and an old-fashioned women's handkerchief lying by the bed. I reached for it but heard footsteps coming up the stairs and only had time to make out two of the three letters monogrammed on the white cloth: a G and an S. Grace Swinton, the woman who hadn't slept in her bed the night of Webber's murder and who looked like her world had ended when Swydecker was whisked away by ambulance. I was now willing to bet my car that she was Swydecker's alibi the night of the murder and he hers, but that neither one of them could risk their careers by coming forth.

Knowing I was on borrowed time, I flew out of the room, my heart thumping in my ears, and rushed to the far end of the second floor walkway a split second before the police officer came into view. If he glared at me, I didn't see. I had my back to him, pretending to knock on Glokkmann's door. I heard a rustle of tape being unwound and glanced to my right, just enough to see that the officer had strung

"Do Not Cross" tape across the entrance to his half of the second story and was doing the same to Swydecker's room.

Meanwhile, on the other side of Glokkmann's door, a howling fight was underway. I heard the crash of glass, a loud thud, and then the most violent sound of all: quiet.

TWENTY

BOTH VOICES WERE FEMALE, but I couldn't recognize either of them and couldn't make out what they had been yelling about. Was Glokk-mann arguing with her daughter, her ostensible roommate whom I had yet to formally meet, and regardless, why hadn't they emerged at the sound of the ambulance and police sirens? I raised my hand to knock. The door opened preemptively, and I found myself face to face with Glokkmann.

"Everything okay?" I asked. She was pale, a slash of red highlighting one cheek.

"Fine." She kept the door tight to her body. "What's all the commotion out here?"

"Swydecker. He was taken away by ambulance." Was I mistaken, or did she not seem surprised?

"Heart attack?"

"Dunno. Grace went with him."

Her eyes narrowed. "I'll have to call her."

We stared at each other. It was still quiet behind her. "You sure everything is okay?"

"I'm sure. I broke a vase. That's all."

A vase? In a hotel room? "I heard another voice."

"The TV."

Short of calling her a liar and pushing her out of the way to see for myself, I had no choice but to leave. Seeing Swydecker gray as ash had taken all the fight out of me. "There's police right down from your room if you decide you need help. Good night." I hurried downstairs, determined to hunt down Bernard and reroute some of my aggression his direction. He wasn't in the lobby, or down by the lake, and when I jogged back to the restaurant, I couldn't find him there, either. My questions for him would have to wait.

———

The next morning, Kennie filled me in via a phone call. Apparently, Swydecker had overdosed. He swore he'd accidentally taken too many of a sleeping pill prescription and hadn't been trying to kill himself. He also claimed that he and Swinton were mere acquaintances by dint of their jobs, and that he hadn't fully latched his door. It must have swung open, which is how Swinton was able to happen across him sprawled on his bathroom floor and called 911. I wondered if he knew about the bridge Mrs. Berns had for sale.

The police had no options other than to treat his story as factual on the face of things, though I knew Wohnt wouldn't let it slide that easily. The good news, for my curiosity anyhow, was that today I'd be interviewing Glokkmann at the library so I could get her angle on the Swydecker situation as well as see if she cared to share anything more about last night's "broken vase."

At home, I was down to condiments, one egg, and slimy lettuce that I'd bought with good intentions. I scratched out a grocery list, wondering why I continued to organize it according to what popped into my head first rather than by meal or what section of the store the ingredients were available in. Micro-evolution eluded me. List made, I herded the animals toward the lake, grabbing a stocking cap and light gloves. The outside thermometer warned me it was only thirty-one degrees, and I wanted to be prepared. The grass crunched underfoot as I stepped onto the lawn, but the sun was already coaxing a melt.

"Want me to bring the frisbee?" Luna's eyes said yes, and we took off toward the lake.

The portion of Sunny's property that abutted Whiskey Lake was not as appealing to me as the thick woods, but I did love the metallic flash of a warming October sun on the surface of open water. Luna followed me down the road that connected my driveway to the driveway of Shangri-La, a woodsy resort located on the peninsula that marked the end of the road. Between my place and Shangri-La was a sandy beach that was all mine. It was a wide spot on the side of the road and anyone going to or from Shangri-La passed right by it, but in the fall, it was quiet.

A rustling in the woods alongside the road alerted me that Tiger Pop was joining us but would not deign to consider herself part of the group. I smiled. The sun felt toasty on my naked cheeks and it wasn't yet 9:00 a.m. That was unusual for mid-October. The last few years, the state had been covered in snow by this time of year. My breath still came out in visible puffs, but the air was redolent with the earthy smell of decomposing leaves rather than the bite of snow approaching from the west.

Most of the leaves still clung to their branches and under the bright eye of the sun, the woods looked like they were ablaze with the reds, oranges, and golds of maple trees against the rich brown of oak leaves and deep green of pine needles. The air smelled like anticipation, like opening a book you were excited to read. Out on the lake far off to my left, a lone fisherman was casting off his boat, a soft breeze waving the lake and gently rolling lapping water onto the shore. I tugged my coat tighter when we reached the edge of the water—it was colder here—and whipped the Frisbee down the road for Luna.

While Luna and I were deep into a game of fetch, Tiger Pop trotted out to sun herself on the dock. I'd need to get some help pulling it in this year. Sunny had written me a letter the previous week informing me that she usually hired a guy named Johnny Leeson to do it, but that anyone in town would be more than willing to help. Yeah, I'll bet she and every other woman in the county wanted to hire a guy named Johnny Leeson. Even the sight of his name made my heart skip, but where we were at now, I didn't know.

I trained my mind back on the moment, the rhythmic game of toss and return with Luna, the soft whisper of the lake, the rustle of wind through dying leaves. It was peaceful, and I absorbed it through my pores. I'd missed this more than anything in the city, the solace of nature. Unfortunately, it was soon time to get to work. I sucked in one last refreshing breath, enough to carry me through the day, and followed the animals back to the house.

I wasn't looking forward to the Glokkmann interview. In fact, all of a sudden, I wanted to wash my hands of the whole ordeal and focus on tending to my fruits and spices, baking, and reading, maybe invite some friends over for a quiet dinner party. Maybe even jump into a relationship with Johnny with my heart fully open to being accepted or being crushed, but open nonetheless. The breeze picked up and blew hair into my face, and I wondered if I could smell a hint of snow after all. I herded Tiger Pop and Luna into the house, reminded them they had a pet door and should keep an eye on each other, and drove to town, vowing that once this murder was solved, I'd embrace all the simple and good things my life offered me.

Glokkmann was waiting for me at the library door, last night's slap mark disappeared from her cheek. She wasn't alone. Standing next to her were Tanya Ingebretson and the dark-haired woman I'd first approached at the debate, the woman who referred to the Representative as "Queen Glokkmann," the woman who I'd been harboring a hunch was Kenya Glokkmann.

"I'm sorry, Sarah. Have you been waiting long?"

She made a show of studying her watch. "I thought you'd be here early now that the library will be opening at ten."

"It's not quite 10:00."

"Aren't there procedures you have to go through first?" Tanya asked. I realized she reminded me of a chipmunk, a tiny, lethal chipmunk, all puffy chest and squat legs, a swirl of brown hair accenting her round, wide-eyed face. She did work hard for Battle Lake, no doubt about it, but she did it to mold us all into her vision rather than out of the goodness of her heart. She'd been a burr under my saddle since I'd arrived, but it wasn't until I'd heard her ridiculous proclamations on gay people that I had a solid reason to dislike her. I wondered if I could start a counter-campaign to deny civil liberties to people who fell in love with wealthy, humorless men named Bud, which happened to describe her husband exactly.

"The library opens at noon. I'm here two hours early as a courtesy to the Representative. I'm sure that will be sufficient time to run through my procedures."

Tanya humphed but didn't press her luck. Glokkmann had already passed me to case the place as soon as I'd opened the door. "This is so charming! One big room. What a wonderful example of how we can do more with less. Do you have sufficient chairs for the reporters?"

I'd driven the long way through town and knew that the parking lots of the motels were again full, the news of Swydecker's suicide attempt bringing in a new rush of bloodthirsty reporters. I was fairly confident Glokkmann had invited any she could track down to today's Q & A.

"Where's Grace?" I asked, disregarding her question.

The dark-haired woman made her first noise, a snort.

Glokkmann spun on her heel. "Mira, please meet Kenya, my daughter. My husband and I adopted her from Korea. We took her in when she was two, so she struggles with attachment disorder."

The cruelty in her words was breathtaking. They had clearly rattled Kenya. Judging by the crafty look on Glokkmann's face, that had been her intention.

"You don't have to tell everyone that, mother. We get it. You're a real humanitarian and I'm a mess." She possessed a striking face, beautiful for its angles and contrasts. She also had a strong body, lean like a dancer, and she carried herself confidently, though I'd already noticed she was more comfortable on the sidelines than the front row. She was dressed professionally in a fitted burgundy cardigan set over pressed black corduroys.

Glokkmann acted as if she didn't hear her. "You know what we could do? We could have the Q & A here in the children's alcove, and the reporters could sit around on the floor like it's story time. That'll show them who's got the upper hand."

Tanya laughed along with her new BFF and pulled out the clipboard that Grace had carried on Tuesday so she could jot down notes.

Centering the Q & A in one of the four corners of the library seemed a straightforward proposition to me, but I suppose it made Tanya feel important to have something to write on a clipboard. She and Glokkmann must have made up.

I cleared my throat. "You didn't mention where Grace was."

"My mother fired her after she found out she was boning the competition," Kenya said, playing with the half pencils at the front counter. Her voice was devoid of emotion.

Her proclamation confirmed beyond a doubt that Grace was the woman who'd been with Swydecker the night of the murder. He must have chosen to protect her rather than clear his name, or I was all wrong about him and he was a cad who didn't want anyone to know he was fooling around on his wife. Regardless, the devastation on Grace's face when she thought she was going to lose Swydecker was evidence of a deep attachment, and that's all I knew for sure.

"That's enough, Kenya! You have to learn when to shut your mouth."

The biting words had an odd effect on Kenya. Her confident posture changed in subtle ways, her shoulders hunching forward and neck swiveling to stare at her mother. Her clear expression went sullen, but she didn't respond. Glokkmann had so far illustrated herself to be more of a chicken-wire momma than an affectionate one, and that must have taken its toll, but there was something darker reflected in her daughter. I wondered how often she'd turned her abusive tongue on her children.

The front doorminder donged, and the reporters began to file in. Tanya directed them to form a half circle around the low-to-the-ground cube chairs that ringed the children's table in the sunny south corner of the library, proud of her authoritative role in front of a potentially national audience. I started to get nervous. I hadn't planned for a crowd when interviewing Glokkmann, and nearly thirty people had streamed in, at least five of them with cameras on their shoulders. They all settled uncomfortably on the floor in a semicircle.

I needn't have worried. All my questions were drowned out by the real reporters who wanted to know about Swydecker and the effect of his attempted suicide on her race to maintain her representative seat, now that she was the shoo-in candidate. Glokkmann rebuffed the questions graciously, answering only when it was to her advantage and even then, sticking to her sound bites. She was a consummate salesperson, and it was hypnotizing. I wouldn't have been able to tear my eyes away if not for the feeling that I was being watched. I ignored the itch until Glokkmann reached for a bottle of water, and then I looked up briefly to see Kenya staring at me, a ghost smile on her lips. I shivered.

"No, I will not be trick-or-treating this Halloween," Glokkmann said to laughter, answering a reporter's question as she set down her water. "Trick-or-treating is a perfect example of how socialism thwarts hard work and innovation. It discourages what would otherwise be a productive and fruitful society."

Off to her left and at the rear of the crowd, I gave her my best what-the-hell face. Was she really equating the blessed tradition of dressing up like monsters and politicians and finagling free candy to socialism? Well, if it was wrong, I didn't want to be right. Unfortunately, Tanya's vigorously agreeing face cancelled out my doubting face, and Glokkmann moved on to the next question. Twenty minutes later, the reporters grew restless, their adult legs not equipped for long stretches of sitting cross-legged on the floor. Glokkmann, ever the reader of her audience, announced the Q & A period at an end and encouraged everyone to look around "this functional example of their tax dollars at work."

Most of them headed straight to the door and so were not present when Gary Wohnt strode through five minutes later in his civilian clothes, sans sunglasses. He could have been any townsperson off the street in to browse the periodicals except for the hell-bent-for-leather expression on his face. It made my chest flutter because I knew from experience that when he looked like that, he usually got what he wanted. Inside the door, he quickly scanned the room, his eyes brushing over me with an almost physical intensity before landing on Sarah Glokkmann, who was trading small talk with one of the few remaining reporters. I grabbed the counter for support, grateful that I wasn't the object of his attention.

He stepped to the side to wait until Glokkmann was finished with her conversation, but he didn't remove his eyes from her person. I took advantage of the rare chance to study him in profile from a safe distance. He had been sort of doughy and repellent before leaving with his born-again tart, but had returned hard and taut, a compact boxer's body under jeans and a button-down white shirt that set off his skin tone beautifully. He reminded me of someone, and I couldn't quite place it. Was it someone I had met in the Cities? Certainly not anyone I'd gone to high school with. Was it some actor?

"Oh my GOD!"

The scattering of people in the library halted their conversations to rubberneck me. I ripped my eyes away from Wohnt, but not before they snapped toward mine with a dangerous glint that spoke of irritation and something muskier.

"I can't believe I forgot my lunch! I was so looking forward to that salad." It was lame but I had to say something because everyone was staring at me and I couldn't say what I was really thinking, which was that Deputy Gary Wohnt, from the side, looked. Exactly. Like. My. Hot Sexy. Unobtainable. Erotic-dream-driving. Chief Wenonga statue.

TWENTY-ONE

My ejaculation changed the mood of the room, which I guess is their nature. The reporters still lingering gave me a wide berth, leaving only Glokkmann and Tanya to side-by-side stare disapprovingly at me. Kenya, I assumed, was off in the stacks along with several regulars who'd been thrilled to find the library open early. Gary took advantage of the break in conversation to stride over to Glokkmann and Tanya. He uttered a few quiet words to Tanya, who blanched before exiting with her purse clutched so tightly I wondered if she had her spare heart in it.

I doubted Glokkmann would pale in the presence of the Grim Reaper himself, but whatever Gary was telling her was making her body stiff. I grabbed the closest object to me, which happened to be a stapler, and strolled over to the table directly behind them and knelt underneath it, pretending to be busy. I presumed that the hair and shoe print in Webber's room had been positively identified, and that Glokkmann was soon going to be kicked off her throne. I wanted to hear it firsthand, though. Unfortunately, Gary was speaking quietly and the only words I caught were "evidence," "reason to believe," and "a scene."

"What're you doing?"

I jumped, and the sudden movement caused me to bump my head on the bottom of the table. "Cleaning."

Kenya crawled next to me and wrinkled her forehead. "With a stapler?"

"I found it under here."

"No you didn't. I saw you carry it over."

"Then I'm stapling the carpet."

"Why?"

For Pete's sake, I couldn't spy on Gary and Glokkmann as long as she was chattering. "Because it was coming loose under the table. Wanna go grab me some staples?"

"Not really. Wanna come by the hotel later and hang?" Her face had returned to its relaxed stage, open and confident.

"Not really."

"Too bad," she said, pulling herself out from under the table and tipping her head at the door. "Because that's probably the only way you'll find out what just happened."

I crawled out from under the table, too, rubbing the goose egg forming on the side of my head. I was just in time to see Gary subtly yet physically escorting the Representative to a waiting unmarked police car.

"I'll be there at seven," I said.

"Great! See you then."

And she skipped out, strangely perky for a woman whose mother has just been arrested. I stood and considered whether it was time to invest in fresh ibuprofen. And then I sneezed twice in rapid succession.

"Gesundheit!" Someone said from the back of the library.

"Thanks," I replied, cursing the cold that was following hot on the heels of my stomach bug. That was all I needed. I blew my nose and made a note to buy myself orange juice and garlic after work. In the meanwhile, I wanted to know what the media knew.

I plunked down at the nearest terminal to see if the police had issued any announcements in the Webber murder and came up empty-handed. Next, I searched for Swydecker and found that the newspapers were reporting him as hospitalized without a specific reason, though the blogs were afire with rumors of a suicide attempt and a mistress. He had not yet officially withdrawn himself from the campaign.

Just to scratch an itch, I did a search on "Glokkmann," "tomatoes," and "Battle Lake" and found a comprehensive story about the drifter who'd pelted her. In a former life, Randall Martineau had been the owner of a small carpet-cleaning business in Glokkmann's district. He'd been forced to close his business when he was struck with an unnamed lung disease and couldn't afford to keep the business afloat and pay his medical bills. Not until he'd given up his business and plummeted to the poverty level did he qualify for state-subsidized health care. His disease was currently in remission and he devoted his time to raising awareness about the health care crisis in the United States. It was Glokkmann's bad luck he and his troupe had landed in Battle Lake this week.

That was enough non-library work for the day. I spent the next several hours helping a young couple figure out how to use the computer to shop for homes in the Cities, locating Otter Tail County records for a researcher from Fargo who was writing his dissertation on Indian burial mounds, browsing *Library Journal* reviews to uncover which books to spend my meager acquisitions funds on, and creating promotional materials for the children's author I had tracked down and booked for a presentation next week. I was about to close up shop at 6:00 when I became aware that I hadn't had time to restack the huge pile of returned books that had accumulated over the day. Sighing deeply, I went to work and checked them in and shelved them in under an hour.

Since I was running late anyway, I stopped by Larry's to buy garlic tabs and orange juice for me and dill pickle potato chips and mineral water for Kenya. Never show up empty-handed, my mother had always taught me. I drank half the carton of juice on the way to the motel and downed three garlic tabs, but the itch in my nose and fogginess in my head were getting worse instead of better. I should just become bubble girl and call it a life.

Pulling into the motel parking lot settled a cold stone in my stomach. I was sick of the place. It was jinxed forward, backward, square, and round, and I would have much rather gone straight home to feel sorry for myself. Unfortunately, my curiosity and obligation to Mrs. Berns were stronger than my self-pity. I trudged up to the lakeside second floor. The police tape was gone, but I'd bet dollars to donuts that neither Swydecker nor Webber's rooms would be occupied anytime soon. In fact, the whole motel felt vacant, except for to my left, where I could hear Rage Against the Machine pumping out of the room that Kenya and Glokkmann shared.

I knocked, then knocked again. I sneezed three times in a row and was about to say "screw you" to my curiosity when the music quieted and the door opened. Kenya was dressed only in a towel, her hair wet. "You're late."

"I'm here now," I said. She was younger than me if only by a year or two, and I wasn't taking any sass from her.

"Hold on, I gotta get dressed." She stepped back from the open door and dropped her towel, making certain to hold my eye contact. I sure wasn't going to look anywhere else; I'd learned that lesson from Darcy.

When I didn't blush or acknowledge her nudity, she turned and strolled over to the dresser. She had a tramp stamp etched on her smooth lower back, ornate words that spelled out something that looked like "non duc duc." I wondered if it was Korean. She had a beautiful body from behind, athletic with curves, but I wasn't a fan of the single white female act. I set down the potato chips and water and walked over to the curtained window, pretending to look out at the lake.

"Tell me when you're done," I said.

She didn't respond. I heard the soft slip of clothing, and then footsteps approaching from behind followed by something furry in my hand. I jumped, and she laughed.

"Don't hurt it!"

I turned to see her holding a fuzzy rodent that she'd tried to slide into my palm. "What the hell is that?"

"A gerbil. His name is Hammy." She set him on the ground and pulled a small gumball-sized rubber ball from the pocket of her silk robe. "Fetch, Hammy!"

"Can he play dead?" I liked rodents a little more than I liked birds.

"No, watch!" The ball disappeared under the bed, and ten seconds later, Hammy scurried out with one cheek bulging. He ran a circle around Kenya before spitting the red ball at her feet.

"Wow." I actually was pretty impressed. I bet I couldn't train my cat to do that, although he wouldn't mind teaching Hammy a trick or two. Actually, just one probably, and it would be called, "tell me what color my stomach is."

"I know! He's my best friend." The creepy seductress was gone and in her place was a young, fresh-faced girl. "He's an absolute genius. Mom hates him. I wish I could bring him everywhere but she makes me leave him in his cage. He hates cages. Would you like living in a cage?"

"No." Her rapid speech made me uncomfortable. "Speaking of your mom, where is she?"

"Grace said that you're a reporter. Do you like reporting?"

"I wouldn't do it for free," I said. "Kenya, did your mom get arrested today?"

"I have a boyfriend, you know. His name is Brad. He's in a rock band."

I sat down across from her. "Kenya, where's your dad at?" I'd initially put her at her mid to late twenties but up close, agitated and without makeup, I wondered if she was even old enough to vote.

"Home. Moorhead."

"Does he know where your mom is?"

She crumpled to the floor and started crying, slow tears that doubled and tripled until she was sobbing. She looked tiny and fragile, and I leaned over to hug her. Hammy scurried up my leg and into her pocket.

"She's in jail! They think she killed that guy, but I know she didn't. She was with me that night. All night. In here."

"All night?" That was what Glokkmann had told the police, but she had no one to corroborate it.

"Yeah." She pulled away and rubbed her hand across her nose. "She was at the Octoberfest thingie for a while. She wanted me with her, you know, so she could do her rainbow nation deal. I played good daughter until I got bored, and then I went to check out the band. That's when I met Brad. Anyhow, she had Grace track me down and said it was time to leave. We all headed back here. Mom took one of her sleeping pills, so an earthquake wouldn't have woken her."

Her story jibed with what Brad had told me. "Did you tell the police that?"

"No." She hung her head. "I was mad at mom for dragging me to this podunk town. I wanted to make her squirm a little, so I told the police I was out all night partying so she wouldn't have anyone to support her story." Her words caught in her throat. "I didn't know they'd arrest her."

"That's what happened today? Your mom was arrested for Bob Webber's murder?"

"Yeah. They said they found some of her hair on the scene. And she didn't have an alibi."

"If you tell them the truth, it will help your mom."

"And land me in jail!"

"It won't look good, but lying to the police about your whereabouts isn't illegal. Right?"

"Will you do it? Go to the police for me, I mean."

"We could go together."

"Haha! Look at Hammy!" He'd peeked out of her pocket and had a piece of lint perched on his nose like a tiny Hitler mustache. "*Sieg heil*, Hammy!"

Her gales of laughter on the heels of torrential tears had my head spinning. Talking to her reminded me of looking through the microscope in ninth grade biology. Everything—oak leaf scales, bacteria, blood platelets—looked like a blurry green eyelash to me. I had to fake it, just like I had to fake that she wasn't screwy.

"Okay, I'll do it, but only if you call your dad and let him know what's up. Plus, the police are going to want to talk to you, so you're only putting this off, not avoiding it altogether."

"Thank you!" She lunged at me with a hug, and I could feel Hammy squirming between us. "I'll call right now." She went over to her purse and yanked out a sparkly pink cell phone.

"No messages," I said.

She gave me the "shush" signal. "Daddy? It's Kenya." She paused, and then started crying again. "The police took her away. And it's all my fault!"

The conversation devolved from there, but toward the end, he must have brought her back on track. She was wiping her eyes and sniffling but sounded okay. "I love you too, Daddy." She hung up the phone. "He's coming. He said he'll be here before the morning to help with mom and to bring me home. I'm sorry I'm so difficult."

"Your life can't be easy." It was the truth. My mother had been an enabler, but she was always there for me. I knew she loved me and was proud of me. Glokkmann had treated Kenya like a trophy when we first met, cutting her daughter down and raising herself in the same stroke. And Glokkmann's treatment of Grace gave me good reason to believe that was just skimming the surface of Glokkmann's dysfunction.

"I'm all right," she said. "I'm just a big baby sometimes. That murder, and then the suicide attempt. And I'm sick of this town. I just want to go home."

"I can sympathize."

She shot me a grateful smile. "I'm fine. But you should probably go. You don't look so good."

I didn't feel so good. My nose felt as red as a cherry, and I could feel a pressure on my lungs. This bug was hitting whatever body parts the previous one had overlooked. "OK. But here's my phone number. Call me if you want me to come back after I talk to the police for your mom. I can stay with you until your dad gets here." I sincerely hoped she didn't call, but I wanted her to know she had options.

"Thanks, Mira. You're a pal."

If by "pal" she meant "village idiot," then we were on the same page. I left with a head full of snot and for the second time in a week would have given any four of my toes to be going home to bed. Instead, I was heading to the Otter Tail County jail in Fergus Falls, a 20 minute drive with the wind at my back.

If you drive in on the east side, Fergus is a bucolic river city, an old village whose downtown has retained much of the charm of turn-of-the-century buildings. The county jail was blocks from this pretty downtown area, a 1987 block of brick appended to the historic, cream-colored limestone and brick courthouse. The only good thing I could say about the jail was that I wouldn't have to run into Gary Wohnt here. I hoped. I was still confused by his electric resemblance to my twenty-three-foot fiberglass love bucket. How could I have not noticed that before? Maybe it was just the lack of sleep and my head cold. Probably Gary didn't look anything like my sweetheart Wenonga. I'd click my heels three times, and the world would return to normal.

I was in luck. Thursday visiting hours were 6:30 to 9:00, which gave me a good fifteen minutes with Glokkmann. I was escorted down industrial hallways to a secured visiting room with rough-clothed couches and bolted-down tables. It reminded me of a high school teacher's lounge. Inside, Glokkmann was seated at a table with a Bible and a handkerchief. I was surprised to see her in the same clothes she'd been arrested in. I assumed she'd be forced to wear a zip-up orange jumpsuit, but here was one more thing *Charlie's Angels* had misinformed me about.

"No interview," she told me, her voice icy. Her hands were clasped tightly in front of her but they still visibly twitched. "I agreed to see you because of my daughter."

"She called?"

"My husband did. He said you'd be on your way."

"Then I'll be brief. Kenya has agreed to tell the police that she was with you the night of the murder."

"The police claim my hair was found tangled in the murdered man's fingers." Her composure was chilling.

"Ick. Did you give them a DNA sample?"

"Not yet."

I'd learned in the past that what the police can accuse you of is completely different than what they can formally charge you with. "Did you kill Bob Webber?"

Her eyes sliced me, fried me, and ate me for supper. "No."

The crapper was, I believed her. I was confident she was a stone cold bitch, but I didn't think she'd murdered Webber. "Look. I know what time period Mr. Webber is believed to be murdered in, and I know you were sleeping during that period. I'm going to tell the police, and Kenya has agreed to substantiate the claim."

I didn't know what emotion I'd been expecting, maybe relief, a little gratitude. Instead, she said, "Fine."

"Fine? I just drove from Battle Lake to help you out. And I have a fever." I might have sounded a little whiny, but I couldn't help it.

"It's not my fault I'm in here."

"It's not mine either."

She held up her nose. "Of course I knew Kenya was in the room with me all night. I was waiting for her to come around and support my story. She's a willful child, but she loses interest in her tantrums fairly quickly." She leaned in closely, her gaze intense. "I love my children. Every one of them. And I will go to the ends of the earth to protect them."

I didn't know what we were talking about, but it was important to her. "You're protecting Kenya? From what?"

"From herself. How much do you know about attachment disorder?"

"Nothing."

"It's common in children adopted between the ages of one and three, at least if they were severely neglected before they were adopted. They have a hard time creating positive attachments and bounce between clingy behavior and distance. They're also manipulative and defiant. Kenya is all these things, and it's because she spent her first two years in an institutional orphanage, the only physical contact once-daily diaper changes and twice-daily feedings. It's made her a difficult person, though she's getting better with medication and therapy. Because of her disorder, she lied about my whereabouts the night of the murder."

I was following, but slowly. "So why didn't you tell the police?"

"Her father and I have spent our lives protecting her, trying to fill the holes in her heart. It's time for her to see the consequences of her actions without our interference."

I wondered if Glokkmann had ever second-guessed a decision she'd made. Some might call it confidence, but from where I was sitting, it was the worst kind of hubris. "So you're letting yourself be put in jail?"

"A mother would understand."

I didn't know why her words stung. "Then you don't need my help."

"I appreciate your coming. This has been a breakthrough for Kenya, it sounds like. She's telling the truth. But no, I don't need you. I can clear myself. The case against me is flimsy, always was."

I'd had exactly enough brain stretching for today. I stood. "Great. Good luck with that."

A horrified expression crawled across her face. She must have assumed that since I'd driven this far that I'd see this pony over the finish line and tell the police what Kenya had said. No reason to waste too much gratitude on me, in that case. But as she realized her miscalculation she stood and gathered her possessions, as if she could leave just as freely as me. I stomped out, stopping on my way only long enough to tell the officer at the front counter what I knew about Glokkmann's alibi, which left me with a clear conscience and absolutely no closer to knowing who had killed Bob Webber.

TWENTY-TWO

THE RING OF THE phone woke me like a slap. Outside my window, the morning was gray, either indicating a crazy early hour or a cool and rainy day. I peeked at my clock before the phone rang a second time: 8:34 a.m. This was a perfectly reasonable time to call, and if it weren't for my head cold, general exhaustion, and the overcast day, I would have been up and about. As it was, I just wanted another ten minutes in bed. Too bad the person on the other end of the phone line didn't know this.

"Hello?" More frog croak than birdsong, but the best I could do.

"Mira James?"

"Yes. Who is this?"

"Glenn Vanderbrick."

Why did that name sound familiar? I wished I wore glasses so I could slide them on now and make the whole world clear. Unfortunately, this was as good as it was going to get. "I'm sorry, who is this?"

"Glenn Vanderbrick. You e-mailed me, asked me to call?"

Now I remembered. He was the guy who'd reserved the room at the motel where Bob Webber's body had been found. I rushed out of bed and into the kitchen for a pen and paper. "That's right! Sorry. Thanks for calling."

"No problem. Did I wake you?"

"Nope." Hardly counted as a lie if it kept someone from feeling bad. "Mind if I ask you a few questions about Bob Webber?"

"I figured that's what this is about. So you're a reporter at *The Recall*?"

"You've heard of us?"

"Not exactly. I picked up a copy of the paper when I was in Battle Lake. Looked good for a small operation." His voice was mellow and deep.

"I'm a part-time reporter."

"Doing a story on Bob?"

"No," I said truthfully. "I was staying in the room next door—next door to the room you were in the night before—and was one of the first people on the scene when he was found. I want to know who killed him."

"The Jacuzzi suite?"

I blushed. "Yes. Any idea how Bob ended up in your room?"

"The police asked me the same thing, and I'm afraid I'm clueless. Bob and I worked on some articles together because we had similar interests and wanted to share research, but we lived in different towns and hung in different circles." His voice grew even deeper. "He was a nice guy. We'd had a drink Friday night and sat next to each other at the Saturday morning debate. That's the last time I saw him."

I replayed the debate. Vanderbrick was the reporter Webber had been talking to after he made his comment about one of the candidates drinking. "Did he say when he was leaving Battle Lake?"

"He said he was checking out Sunday morning. I told him I was staying until Saturday around eight because I had a lead that Glokkmann would make official her future run for governor that night. When he caught wind of that, he booked his room for another night. She never did, of course, and I left for home around 6:00 that Saturday. Never saw Webber that whole day after the debate."

That explained Webber's length-of-stay alteration on the cleaning lady's room list. He was the one who had changed the date of his stay and likely the motel staff had modified the list. "So Bob hadn't even been in your room when you were there?"

"Nope. Nor I in his."

Another dead end. "Not to be rude, but you have a witness for where you were Saturday night?"

"About 300," he said. "There was a gaming convention in the Cities that I was at that night. We played Magic: The Gathering all night."

Pretty airtight. What was I missing? "Any idea who might have done Bob in?"

"I don't like to make accusations I can't support, but I do know that Representative Glokkmann wasn't running for president of his fan club. Other than that, no idea."

"I checked out *The Body Politic*. Why was Bob the only one in the media to pick up on Glokkmann's dirty dealings?"

"*Was* is the operative word there. He had a source on Glokkmann's campaign, don't know who, and that person gave him the dirt. Nothing he could prove, though, and it wasn't ever a big enough story for the straight news to risk a libel case over. That was until he got killed. Now everybody with a computer and two fingers is digging into Glokkmann's business. If Bob was right about her taking bribes and drinking herself into an early grave, his murder is the worst thing that could have happened to her."

That jibed with what my instincts were telling me. Glokkmann didn't kill Webber. She might be small-minded, but she wasn't stupid. Whoever killed the blogger did it to hurt her, and I could think of four people right off the top of my head who'd like a piece of that pie: Swydecker, Swinton, Kenya, and Randy Martineau. Swydecker was the most obvious suspect. Glokkmann stood in the way of his fulfilling his life dream. And, he'd just tried to kill himself, which was the action of a man with tremendous guilt. Swinton must have a great deal of inner conflict working for Glokkmann while sleeping with her opponent, too, but was it enough to kill? I thought it more likely that she was Webber's informant, though maybe that entanglement had led to murder.

Kenya did not strike me as mentally well, but if she wanted to hurt her mom, there were much easier ways than committing murder. She surely could gain access to Glokkmann's financial information as well as her personal secrets. Randy Martineau was a wild card. He was in the motel parking lot the morning after the murder, and he had an axe to grind against Glokkmann. I couldn't see a guy switching from murder to tomato-throwing, though. Too inconsistent. And I hadn't even thrown Bernard Mink into the mix. I still didn't know why he hadn't liked Webber, but I did know he had a hot temper. So who'd killed the blogger?

"It makes sense that someone out to get Glokkmann would have killed Webber. You know she's in jail, right?"

"Again, *was*," he said, not unkindly. "Her lawyers sprung her last night. The case against her was weak."

"Oh." Must be nice to be a real reporter who actually knew stuff.

"Anything else you want to know?"

"Yeah. How can you bloggers afford high-end motel rooms?"

He laughed. "It's the future of news. You should look into it. Do some freelance work. You can actually make money."

"I might take you up on that. Can I call you if I have more questions?" He said yes, and we exchanged information and said our goodbyes.

I returned the phone to its cradle, nursing a feeling that the only way to find the killer would be to discover why Bob Webber was in room 19 Saturday night. But how to do that? I couldn't ask Webber, obviously. I also didn't know anything about his family and didn't feel comfortable tracking them down to bother them in their time of grief. I could always scour his blog one more time searching for a clue among his posts, maybe an in-progress investigative piece that I hadn't read closely enough. Anything that would have called him to room 19 of the Big Chief Motor Lodge would have been related to Battle Lake. Had I been overlooking something in focusing on the political candidates because the room Webber's body was found in was on the same floor that Swydecker, Swinton, and Glokkmann were staying on? What if Webber had met someone at the Octoberfest celebration and they had rendezvoused in a room that Webber knew would be empty, and their illicit activities had taken a dark turn? Dangnabbit, I'd have to call Kennie again to find out what else she knew. It seemed like I was missing something obvious, and I still felt that way when I pulled into the library to start my Friday shift. At least my head cold seemed to be clearing.

I squeezed my sleuthing to the side to prepare the library for children's hour, my most favorite library event of the week. Some days up to a dozen kids showed, from diaper-bound toddlers to preschool-aged. The boys inevitably smelled like farts and stowed at least one plastic toy in each pocket. The girls were bossy and cute. Although it didn't give me much hope for the procreation of the species, it was glorious to bask in the open and honest joy of the children.

They loved when I employed different voices to tell the stories. When I dropped to all fours to act out a wolf sneaking up on a sheep, they squealed. If the book had a joke that involved someone's pants falling down, they laughed until their faces were red and wet with tears. I wished I could bag them all up and bring them home with me, but I bet they were a lot of work if you had to tend to their needs for more than an hour a week.

My reading selections for today were *Peaceful Piggy Yoga* because I thought they'd get a hoot out of practicing yoga positions while I read, *Don't Let the Pigeon Drive the Bus* because it was an awesome book and I'd had a tough week, *But Not the Hippopotamus* because they loved the silly, cheerful pictures, and *You Think It's Easy Being the Tooth Fairy?* because a couple of my regulars had some loose front lower teeth that they were holding onto like gold.

My books stacked, I finished some odds and ends in preparation. I was just throwing out the too-stubby coloring crayons from the art bucket I kept on hand when in strolled Elizabeth Berns.

"I hope I'm not bothering you."

I looked from the stack of books to her and decided I might as well be gracious. "I suppose not." I didn't say I was good at it.

"Can I talk to you?"

"Yeah, I've got a minute. Is it about your mom?"

She fiddled with her expensive-looking amber bracelet. "Conrad wants her admitted to the new home before Halloween."

My heart hardened. "What? I thought you two were going to monitor her for a little bit first, get a feel for her day-to-day life."

"I wanted to, but Conrad said there isn't time. He thinks she's marrying that Bernard guy so she won't get sent away and that we better move fast or we won't have any say in her life."

Was there steam coming out of my ears? I was too angry to even speak.

"I know how that sounds, believe me I do. Conrad and I fighting her fiancé for control of her life."

"Then why'd you say it?"

"Can I tell you a story?" She smiled uncomfortably. "When I was a little girl, my mom was my hero. Life wasn't easy but she always made time to read to us, sewed beautiful clothes for us, and made the best from-scratch food in the county. She was famous for her buttermilk biscuits. They were rich and crusty, and we'd smother them in her homemade raspberry jam. When I was eight, my brothers and sisters and I decided we were going to make those biscuits for her for Mother's Day. She would get breakfast in bed." Elizabeth's eyes grew sad.

"What happened?"

"We ruined them, of course, and almost burned down the kitchen in the process. Dad, bless his Swedish heart, was livid. He yelled at mom for being foolish enough to let a bunch of little kids cook. She had to spend the rest of the day scrubbing the soot off the wall and cleaning her kitchen and cookware. We never ventured in her kitchen again, even though she didn't say one mean word to us. In fact, she thanked us kindly for trying to make a special morning for her. Don't you see? How could I forgive myself if I let something happen to that woman?"

A frustrated tear leaked out the edge of Elizabeth's eye, and I realized in a rush of joy that she'd already made up her mind, had, in fact, made it up before she'd walked in the door. She wasn't going to sign the papers, but she needed me, someone who knew and loved her mom as she was now, to convince her it was okay. "You and your family are very lucky," I started tentatively. "Your mother sounds like she had a level head."

Elizabeth pulled a tissue out of her purse and nodded.

"She still does, despite her escapades," I continued. "I can't promise she'll be fine, because I can't promise that about anyone. I can tell you that she's happy, and that sending her away would ruin her."

"Do you think she loves Bernard?"

"No," I said honestly. "I think she's just marrying him to get you and Conrad out of her hair."

Elizabeth sniffled. "Are we that bad?"

I raised my eyebrows. They're my best feature when it comes to conveying judgment.

"Don't be too hard on us. Conrad means well. It was hardest on him to lose Dad, and then to feel like he didn't know his mom anymore. He's been trying to fix that ever since Dad passed, to bring back the mom he remembers."

"Don't help him to force his needs on Mrs. Berns."

"I won't," she said, drawing in a shaky sigh. "But I've got to figure out how to tell Conrad that."

"The direct route is the best." At least that's what I'd read.

"Thanks, Mira. I mean it. My mom really loves you, and I know you've done a lot for her. I wish … never mind."

"What?"

"It's silly. I just wish I had the type of relationship with her that you do. I suppose I live too far away."

"Not today, you don't. Take her out for a night on the town. If you start out by telling her that you're not sending her up the river, I bet you two'll have a great time."

She smiled. "Probably I should wait until I've convinced Conrad to let her stay in Battle Lake. You have a good day, and thank you. I mean that."

She gave me a hug and left me feeling relieved. If she could convince Conrad that Mrs. Berns was not mentally incompetent, then Mrs. Berns wouldn't need to get married. That put me into all sorts of good mood, and as the children began strolling in, I high-fived each one of them and led them to a spot on the reading circle. In about ten minutes I had the group settled on the floor, their mothers and one father looking exhausted but hopeful, when in walked Kenya.

She plopped down at the outskirts of the circle. "Oh good! I was hoping I'd make it."

"This is for kids," Walter, the child nearest her, exclaimed. He was three years old but would swear he was four if you asked.

"I know! I love children's stories. Do you mind if I stay?"

And the children, with their blanket acceptance, all agreed she was perfectly welcome to stay and would be even more welcome if she happened to have some loose candy on her. She didn't.

I began the story, not as accepting as the kids. Kenya was a click off of normal, and I didn't like her imposing on my happy place. Still, she did look bright-eyed and turned out to be gifted with children, helping them to achieve the down dog and stretching cat poses and redirecting their attention to me when Walter accidentally tooted during the frog pose. By the time story hour was over, she had two children in her lap and another one braiding her hair.

A few kids stayed after to read books with their parents, but most of them cleared out for lunch and naptime. Kenya stayed after.

"Hope it didn't bother you that I showed," she said. "I saw the flyer for kids reading time when I was here yesterday. I love kids. I'd love to open a daycare someday, actually."

"Why don't you?"

Yesterday, she'd seemed on drugs, and today she was sane as a judge. I decided there's be no percentage in commenting on her mood swings.

She made a grimace. "My parents say it'd be a waste of a good brain. I'm studying engineering at the University of North Dakota."

"Maybe you could engineer a daycare?"

She laughed at my lame joke. "I wanted to thank you, too."

"For what?"

"For being so nice to me yesterday, and for helping me to see the light. I'm getting a little old to be rebelling against my parents, you know? My mom was released from jail last night, and we had a good talk. She seems like she's learned a little humility. My dad couldn't make it yet—the insurance business is booming, you know—but the police said we can go back to Moorhead tomorrow morning. No offense, but it'll be a relief to be back with my friends, and even back in my stupid classes."

"The police are letting you go home?"

"Well, they could never officially hold us, except for when mom was in jail. They just asked for our cooperation in staying close, and mom has to always be a friend to the law. Whoops! There I go again. Old habits die hard. She was probably right that it was best for everyone that we stayed around while they looked for the killer."

"They still don't know anything?"

"Not that I know. Hold on." She reached into her pocket to pull out her vibrating cell phone. She smiled at first, and then her mouth drooped, and then it looked like she had been stabbed, all the blood drained from her face so fast. She dropped the phone and stood there, staring toward nothing.

I put out my arm to catch her. "What is it?"

"My mom. She's dead."

TWENTY-THREE

I ENTREATED ONE OF the mothers to watch the library until Mrs. Berns could arrive, and then I drove Kenya to the motel as fast as I could. She was silent the whole way, staring straight ahead as if she were sleepwalking. I felt like I should reach out to her but didn't know what to say. We pulled up to the familiar sight of police cruisers and an ambulance in the motel parking lot.

Kenya hadn't remembered to wear her jacket from the library, and it was cold out. I wrapped my coat around her to ward off the brisk lake wind driving waves onto shore with white-capped ferocity, even though she seemed oblivious to the temperature. Gary Wohnt was the first to spot us and strode over to take Kenya off my hands, not even bothering to shoot me a look before leading her off to his car, where he had her sit half in and half out and offered her coffee.

I stayed close by.

"I'm sorry," he told her gruffly. She didn't acknowledge the coffee he was offering her, and he set it on the roof of his car before continuing. "Your father called you?"

She nodded.

"He should be here shortly. It looks like your mother committed suicide. We found a note on the scene."

She looked at him timorously. "Can I see it?"

"I'm afraid not. We're treating this as a crime scene until we know exactly what happened."

Kenya began sobbing, deep hiccups of sadness. I stood there feeling helpless until I spotted Bernard Mink skulking along the perimeter, a tiny tape recorder shoved against his mouth. I told a blank-faced Kenya that I would be back and snuck up on Bernard from behind.

"Whatcha doing?"

He jumped and turned. His bruise had become an ugly green-yellow. "Fuck off."

I was completely appalled. I'd meant to annoy him, sure, payment in kind. I hadn't expected to be met with crude anger. I feared I was looking at the true Bernard Mink. "You can't talk to me like that!"

"Looks like that's one more thing you're wrong about."

"What's the other thing?"

"Go away."

"You go away. I'm only here because I'm trying to clear your ugly name in the murder of Bob Webber."

He glanced back toward the second floor to the open door of Glokkmann's room. "Not necessary. She 'fessed up. In her note."

"To killing Webber?"

"Among other things."

"How do you know?" Jeezus, the man pissed me off.

"Good reporting is about being at the right place at the right time. Plus, the officer over there is my sister's husband and he was the first one on the scene."

Crap. If his brother-in-law had told him what was in Glokkmann's suicide note, he probably told him a lot more. It's a cracking shame that curiosity is such a hard taskmaster. It made me beg this creep for answers. "Who found her body?"

"Cleaning lady."

I grimaced. "That woman should get a raise."

He ignored me. "They clean rooms a little after lunch for extended stays. Glokkmann's body was barely cold when she walked in on it."

"How'd she do it?"

"Who?" He was starting to walk away from me.

"Glokkmann, of course. How'd she kill herself?"

"Gun. Pretty messy, I hear. Can't imagine this motel will stay open much longer."

"No, me neither," I mumbled as he walked off to talk to the man I presumed was his brother-in-law. Glokkmann's death didn't sit right, and it wasn't just the gruesome manner in which it had been executed. Webber had been murdered in a way that looked like suicide, and then Swydecker had attempted suicide in a stereotypically feminine way while Glokkmann had offed herself with a gun, a rare choice for women. What other connections did all three share?

I returned to Kenya's side. Wohnt still had his eyes on her, though her sobbing had subsided. "I can stay with her until her dad shows up."

His eyes flashed at me, and for a second, I thought I saw gratitude.

Kenya didn't want to talk, and so I retrieved a blanket from my car and sat with her on the motel's lakeshore deck until her father showed up two hours later. He was a handsome man in his mid-fifties, trim with salt and pepper hair and wearing a suit that had probably started out the day neatly pressed but now looked grieved in. He ran up to his daughter and held her tightly. They both cried, and it about broke my heart. I had actively disliked Glokkmann, but she had people who loved her as a wife and mother, and their sorrow deserved respect.

Seeing Kenya in good hands, I dragged myself back to my car. I smelled something familiar next to it, maybe a combination of BO and tomatoes, but I didn't see any sign of the drifter. Probably just something washed up on shore.

TWENTY-FOUR

I DIDN'T KNOW WHERE to go after I left Kenya, so I returned to work, craving a drink more than I had since I'd quit in September. It was a physical pain, a heartache that could only be cauterized by the hot sear of liquor gliding down my throat. Watching Kenya cry, I'd been reminded of my sad, sixteen-year-old self the day I'd found out my dad had died in the car accident. My first reaction had been shock, a term that doesn't do justice to the feeling that all of you has been shrunk to the size of an eye, with no body to hold, no legs to run away on, the world a wild spinning place, dangerous to a tiny, wet eye. All you can do is see without comprehending and remain in constant motion to stay safe.

My shock wore off before my mom's, and I spent the next few days sitting by her bedside as people came and went with casseroles and murmured sympathy. I don't remember crying. I recalled guilt over my relief, but no tears. I'd seen that same shock in Kenya, and while she had the humanity to sob in the face of her mother's death,

I'd also spied a flash of relief in her eyes, and I understood. I hoped she would go easier on herself than I had.

I steered past the library and all the way to the south end of town, pulling into the Municipal Liquor Store parking lot. Nobody needed to know I'd had a drink. Actually, who would care? I was an adult. I'd only be letting myself down. Stepping out of my car, I wondered whether I should be civilized and buy a bottle of red wine, or be honest and buy vodka. I chose the vodka. I almost didn't stop at the library on my way back. Mrs. Berns knew how to close up and could do fine on her own. The vodka, on the other hand, needed me.

The yellow brick called to me as I passed, though, and reminded me that I didn't know whether or not Mrs. Berns had actually made it in. The vodka could wait ten minutes. I twitched into the parking lot and pulled into my Reserved for Librarian space. Walking toward the library entrance, I counted six cars in the paved lot, two of them minivans. Outside, the potentilla shrubs clung to a last bit of color, but I'd need to trim them and clean the cigarette butts from the rock garden before the first snows hit. There'd be time.

A feeling of utter relaxation seeped into my bones. I knew how I'd be spending tonight, and it felt good. Just had to make sure the library was in capable hands, and I'd go home and check out for the night.

"You get laid?"

"What?"

Mrs. Berns was sitting on a rolling chair in the center of the library with her cast propped in front of her on another chair. She was painting her free toenails a hot pink. "I asked if you'd gotten some action. You've got a goofy look on your face, and you either got laid or you're…" Her eyes sharpened. "Go get it."

"Get what?" I'd already started backing toward the door.

"The bottle."

"I don't know what you're talking about." That was the wrong answer. I always knew what she was talking about, even if I didn't want to, and Mrs. Berns was fully aware of that fact.

"You're going to make a crippled old lady get off this chair and fight you for a bottle of wine?"

"Vodka."

"That bad, huh?"

"How'd you get here anyhow?"

"Well, I can tell you for sure that gravity didn't lend a hand." She capped the bottle of polish and blew on her toenails. "I'm trying out this color for my wedding. What do you think?"

"Looks fine."

"From there, yeah, but come close so you can see it from my perspective."

I strode over and peered at her toes. "A little bright, but nice."

Smack. She whacked me across the top of the head.

"What'd you do that for?" She'd hit the same spot I'd bonked on the underside of the table when trying to spy on Wohnt and Glokkmann.

"Because you're a dumbass. Things get tough and you go back to drinking? I never understood why you were giving it up in the first place, but since it was your choice, you'd think you'd have a little more backbone about it."

I rubbed my head. "Sarah Glokkmann killed herself this morning."

"I know."

"Her daughter looked crushed."

"You'd expect that."

My eyes felt hot. "It's just a lot to process, you know? That's two deaths and a suicide this week alone. And now, there's a girl without a mother."

She squinted at me. "That must be tough, losing a parent."

"Yeah." The heat in my eyes was turning wet.

"Probably make somebody a big baby forever."

"Most likely."

"Come here." And she pulled me to her and held what parts of me she could reach in a surprisingly tight hug, squeezing more tears out of me than I knew I possessed. She patted while she held me and didn't let up until the tears stopped. "Are you better?"

"Yes." I didn't want her to let go. Up close, she smelled like old-fashioned lipstick and fresh bread.

"Then get off of me. Hey, Harold!"

I glanced behind to see an uncomfortable-looking Harry Lohwese trying to sneak out of the library.

"Don't worry," Mrs. Berns said. "The crying isn't contagious. Mira here just found out she's allergic to vodka, right after she bought a bottle. Do us a favor and take it off her hands. It's the brown Toyota out there, doors are open."

He nodded happily and walked out. I took advantage of the break to blow a pound of snot out of my nose. "Thanks."

"You want to thank me, you find the killer."

"Done. Glokkmann confessed to it in her suicide note. Bernard didn't come tell you?"

She appeared momentarily flustered but covered well. "He's his own man, not p-whipped like your Johnny. So, the representative killed the bobber after all."

"Blogger."

"Gesundheit."

I sighed. "Thank you. Can I ask you something? I haven't gotten a chance to ask Bernard, but what did he do to land in jail in the first place?"

"Bar fights, mostly, with a few DWIs thrown in for flavor. He's got a temper on him when he drinks."

I considered the police blotter I'd uncovered and his rude outburst at the motel today. It wasn't just when he drank. "He drink around you?"

"Not often."

"He's doesn't deserve you." I reached into my purse and fished out the print-outs from the *Daily Register*. "He's got problems."

She scanned the paper. "You think I don't know all about this?"

"Do you?"

Her shoulders drooped. "Well, not this exactly, but I'm not blind to his issues." She sighed and looked me in the eye. "Fine. I didn't tell you the whole story. We've got a business arrangement, Bernard and I. The plan is that he and I party together for a few weeks, get married, and Conrad loses interest in having me declared mentally incompetent. Then, Bernard and I get divorced, I pay him $5,000, and I never see him again."

I whistled through my teeth. "So why Bernard?"

"That's all I had time for. He and I first met in the gas station, like I told you, and we had a couple weeks of fun. Then Conrad shows up, and I have to quick-like unearth a fiancé. Bernard was convenient. He's got poor character, it's true, but that makes him easier to bribe and it means he knows how to keep a secret. The bobber's death almost ruined it all, but it looks like that's been cleared up, too."

"I never did get a chance to ask Bernard why he and Webber didn't get along."

"Professional rivalry, near as I can tell. It's just that when you're on probation for an assault charge, and the man you'd happened to publicly threaten at a certain small-town beer festival shows up dead the next day, you like to cover your tracks." Her toenails dry, she pulled on her sock and tennis shoe.

I chose my words carefully. "Elizabeth came to see me today."

"I know."

"How?"

"She came by afterward, told me that she wasn't going to sign off on the mental incompetency papers." She looked serious.

"Well, yeah! That's great news, isn't it?"

"She said she didn't feel close to me anymore."

"Oh." I considered returning the hug. "She does live far away."

"That shouldn't matter."

"So what're you going to do?"

A glint sparkled deep in her eyes. "I'm going on vacation. Ever been to Sedona?" She pronounced every syllable. *C-doe-na.*

"Nope."

"I hear there's a lot of sugar daddies there."

I smiled hopefully. "That mean you're not getting married? You wouldn't have to anyways, now that your kids are off your back."

"Just one kid. Conrad is still behaving like a coonhound with shit on his nose, and he could talk another one of my fool kids into putting me away at any time."

"So you're going through with the wedding, even though you know Bernard has a violent temper and a possible drinking problem?"

"You're no better than my kids, trying to control me like that. It's a business arrangement, I told you. Bernard has weak moral fiber, which makes him perfect for a shotgun, short-term marriage. He'll serve his purpose, and I'll be a free old lady once again." Mrs. Berns reached for her crutches. "Now help me up. I've gotta get going now that you're back."

I was resigned to respect her decisions as much as they worried me. I'd have to let her accept the consequences of her decision, though you'd better bet your bumper that I'd be keeping a close eye on Bernard until the divorce was signed and he was out of town for good. "How're your ribs feeling?"

"Cracked. I'll be sad when the bruises fade, though. They make me look street tough."

I studied her green and blue face affectionately. "You look tough all right." I helped her stand up, surprised at how feather light she was. "Now where are you off to? Or is it, 'to where are you off?' I always forget where to put the preposition."

She rearranged her clothes before picking up her crutches. "I find that if I toss in some profanity, it throws people off so they don't even think about the grammar. 'Where the hell are you going?' See how that works?"

"Yes. Thank you."

"You're welcome. And I'm going to finish my wedding planning. Bernard is picking me up out front."

I watched her limp away. "Need help?"

"No offense, but you're not exactly the go-to person for girlie stuff like wedding planning."

"None taken." And she left me, still feeling a little sad and shaken but gratefully whole.

TWENTY-FIVE

THE NEXT TIME I saw Kenya she looked more shattered than when I'd left her on the shore of West Battle. It was Sunday morning, and she was in a pew at the Henning Catholic Church for her mother's funeral. Outside, an icy rain shot needle-like against the church walls, the sky as gray and cold as stone. Hordes of media held umbrellas against the barrage, breathing white puffs of chilly air. From above, they would look like a clot of black lily pads in a slate-colored pond.

Friends and family were allowed to enter the church early to escape the cold, but the thronging press was forbidden inside. Kennie, distastefully dressed in a black bandage dress and stiletto heels, had confirmed in a loud whisper at the back of the church that Bernard Mink was correct and Sarah Glokkmann had confessed in writing to the murder of Bob Webber before killing herself. The autopsy required in Minnesota in cases of violent death showed that she had died of a self-inflicted gunshot wound to the head, as indicated by the range and angle of the shot as well as the powder residue on her right hand. It was too soon to know what the results of her toxicology screen were, but the medical examiner didn't expect to find anything unusual.

"How do they know it was her handwriting on the note?" It just didn't sit right. I knew Glokkmann hadn't killed Webber. Didn't I?

"They've got experts for that." She adjusted her three-story hat. She looked straight out of a gothic Kentucky Derby.

"How is anybody supposed to see around that monstrosity?" I asked her. "And why'd you come, anyway?"

"I went to school with Sarah."

"You didn't like her any more than I did."

She reached back to scratch her ankle. The fishnets must be itchy. "You shouldn't speak ill of the dead. Did you see how many people are here? We're lucky we came early."

"Yeah, some people had to camp out for tickets," I said wryly. "Why didn't you like her?"

She pursed her lips. "It's old news."

"I'm feeling old today. Enlighten me."

"She wore the same dress as me to prom."

"What?" I couldn't help a small chuckle. If humans aren't the most ridiculous animal on the planet, with their petty grudges and their magpie-like need to accumulate, I didn't know what was.

"She knew I'd already bought it," she said haughtily. "A strapless, seafoam pink gown with a matching capelet."

"Seafoam isn't pink."

"It is when you buy it in Otter Tail County. And she had a professional style her hair. I couldn't compete with that. I had to do my hair myself. She ruined the night for me."

"It's good you've been able to put this in perspective and attend her funeral."

"Exactly," she said, smoothing her dress and looking expectantly at the front door. I think she was hoping one of the national news crew would forego the rules and crash the church.

"So, word around town is that the Big Chief Motor Lodge is closing at the end of this month."

She nodded. "As mayor, I hate to see a new business fold, but that place was jinxed. Two attempted suicides, one successful, and a murder? All in one week? Plus, the place had mice."

My attention was drawn to Kenya at the front of the church, breaking away from her family to sit alone in a pew. She looked broken. "You don't know that."

"Do too. Saw the turds myself. All over the murdered man's room. Can't imagine what the rest of the place looked like. The luck there was so bad, it was probably built on a snake's nest."

I'd seen a news clip a couple years ago about a whole development in a suburb of Minneapolis built above snake nests, swarming live balls of hundreds upon hundreds of baby snakes. The owners couldn't figure out how the reptiles kept getting into their houses until one woman tried to plant a garden and tilled up squirming snakes. The mere thought of it was enough to make me want to buy stilts. "Probably. Catch you later."

"Fine."

I sauntered toward the front of the gorgeous church, admiring the blue and gold stained glass window. The profusion of fresh flowers was overwhelming in perfume and color. As I neared the flowers, my head cold, which seemed to be clearing up yesterday, came back at me with a vengeance. I'd told Kenya I would visit with her at the funeral, so I persevered. Her sisters and brothers had surrounded each other for the pre-service, and this was the first moment we'd had to talk. I slid in next to her.

She turned toward me with sad brown eyes. "You know on Friday when I said I'd finally be getting out of this place? I was wrong."

I tried to for lightness. "Henning is completely different than Battle Lake."

"Coulda fooled me."

"You're going home after the funeral?"

"After the burial. Mom's family is all laid to rest out here, and this is where she and dad bought their plots. Gruesome, I think, to buy that stuff in advance."

I shrugged. "One less thing for you to worry about. How's your dad holding up?"

"As well as can be expected, I suppose. You know they were high school sweethearts? They still held hands."

"I'm sorry." I sneezed twice and grabbed for a tissue. I felt like I had fiberglass under the skin of my face. "Can I ask you something completely unrelated? What's your tattoo say?" The curiosity hadn't been killing me, but it had been sending threatening notes.

She smiled a murmur of a smile. "You saw my tattoo?"

"Yeah. Hard to miss."

"*Non ducor duco.*"

"What's it mean?"

"It's Latin: 'I am not led; I lead.'"

I sneezed again, but with this one came an oily tingle down my back. There was danger near, something not right. Before I could pinpoint it, I saw movement in the front of Kenya's shapeless black dress. Both her hands were out where I could see them. "Kenya, did you bring Hammy?"

She giggled quietly and slipped her hand into her pocket, pulling out a brown ball of fuzz. "Don't tell."

Suddenly, the world tilted a little. Kenya's profile was in sharp relief and I could see every pore on her face. I wondered if this is what it felt like to learn you've been poisoned, this sudden onset of horrific awareness. I knew who had killed Bob Webber, and it wasn't Sarah Glokkmann.

TWENTY-SIX

SITTING THROUGH THE FUNERAL service was a trying experience, and I wouldn't have done it except I had promised, and I knew the killer wasn't going anywhere. Still, I fidgeted so much next to Kennie that she pinched me hard enough to draw blood. That served to make me crabby on top of the fidgety. The only thing that stilled me was when Grace Swinton entered the church after the priest had begun to speak, selecting a seat at the end of the back row Kennie and I had been relegated to. She was beautifully put together, wearing a crisp green suit that set off her eyes and hair. Her face was drawn and pale, her skin like porcelain. She wrung her hands nervously as she sat but was otherwise motionless.

After the priest's initial words, Kenya's dad stood and walked painfully to the podium. He brought out a piece of paper, his hands shaking, but forwent reading it. Instead, he told stories about first setting eyes on his wife in kindergarten and knowing even then that he'd marry her, about her commitment to her community and her faith in God, about how much she loved each of her children and would be looking down on them from Heaven. Two of the children spoke after that, followed by friends and colleagues. The priest asked if anyone else had words they wanted to share, and Grace began to stand before falling heavily into her seat, tears streaming from her eyes. I felt bad for her.

Finally, after some hymns and psalms, the service was over. The priest invited those present to join the family at the burial, immediately followed by dinner in the church basement. I'm ashamed to admit I loved church basement food. Salty turkey slices on buttered white rolls, noodle hotdish, baked beans, orange Jell-O and pineapple salad with carrot strips, potato chips and pickles, red juice, and lemon bars. I'd have to skip this one, though, because I had a murderer to catch.

The rain was still pelting the stained glass of the windows, so I stepped toward the door of the basement rather than follow Kennie out the church. I hated being pressed in a slow-moving crowd, and if I waited, the needle rain might let up. I held a placid smile on my face, idly watching the huge crowd shuffle out the church.

"Mira."

Turning, I spotted Grace in the shadow of one of the confessionals. I strode over to her. "Are you okay?"

Her eyes were bloodshot and puffy. "I was the one who told Webber about Sarah's ethical breaches. I did it. It was me."

"I know."

She wasn't listening. She'd uncovered this geyser of guilt and couldn't stop the surge. "It was all true, but I didn't want anyone to get hurt. I just couldn't live with myself if I let her get away with taking bribes and drinking herself into the ground. I see you judging me."

I averted my gaze.

"I'd judge me, too. I can't stand bribes and alcoholism but don't have a problem with adultery? I'm not going to make excuses. I loved Arnold, and it was wrong."

"How is he?"

"Fine. He's a good man, the best. He decided he couldn't live with what he'd done, but he doesn't think that anymore. He's going to go to counseling." A sob escaped. "With his wife."

I reached out to her, but she pulled away. "No, no, this is what I deserve. I need you to know something, though. Sarah Glokkmann was a fighter. She would never kill herself." She grabbed my upper arm, her fingers like a steel trap. "Listen to me. She didn't kill herself."

An icy tongue licked between my shoulder blades. Grace's words had the ring of truth. This added a layer of urgency to my actions. I gave her a quick hug and darted out a side door of the church, ignoring the sleet and milling crowds to dash to my car.

I knew my case was precarious, so I did my research first, stopping on my way back from the funeral to talk to Darcy and Cindy. They'd stopped by the library twice since I'd introduced them, all blissed out on new love and searching for books on everything from horse grooming to rabbit care. They'd been together all of three days before they were finishing each other's sentences. On the last visit Cindy had given me her phone number, telling me that she and Darcy wanted to take me out to thank me for bringing them together. I'm surprised I'd hung onto it. Being forced to witness the saccharine glow of new love appealed about as much as licking dirt.

I was glad I had, and as I pulled up to Cindy's 1970s-era rambler and knocked on her door, I was also grateful that they were around on a Sunday afternoon.

"OK, guys, I have a weird question? Um, guys?" They had greeted me nicely enough and ushered me into the spacious living room but were now staring deeply into each other's eyes. To make it even worse, Cindy was a doll collector, and had two full China cabinets of glass-faced horrors on each side of the room watching me, noting my weaknesses, moving slowly just out my line of vision.

"Sorry," Cindy said, blushing. "What's the question?" Darcy whispered something in her ear and she giggled.

I looked at her in desperation. PDA + doll collection = I needed to get out of this house before my eyes combusted. "I think I'm allergic to gerbils. How would I tell?"

"That's very..." Darcy said.

"...common," Cindy finished.

I held up a hand. "One at a time."

Cindy stepped up to the plate. "Gerbils are similar to cats in that they have a protein in their urine and saliva that people can be allergic to. They clean their fur, the protein gets on the fur, they shed the fur. If you're sensitive, you might get headaches, itchy eyes, and sneezing."

I nodded. It was exactly what I'd suspected. "Would it take a whole army of gerbils to set this off, or would one be good enough to do it?"

"Depends how sensitive you are," Darcy said. "Come on down."

And they welcomed me into Cindy's basement, which looked like Noah's Ark had crashed into Dr. Doolittle's island. She had one of everything—lizard, bunny, frog, even a disagreeably beady-eyed parakeet. I thought they'd been playing one of those soothing sounds of nature soundtracks when I arrived, but it turned out they had the real deal going on.

"How come it doesn't smell down here?" I asked before my social filter clicked in.

"I figure they want to live as cleanly as I do," Cindy said. "I spend a lot of time cleaning bedding. Now I have Darcy to help me." They exchanged eye syrup and dopey smiles. "Follow me."

I sidestepped the bird, holding my fingers over my face like the bars of a cage to remind him who had the power. Cindy led me to the bunny pen and reached out to hand me a soft, warm puff of white.

"It's shaking," I said.

"Pet it like this." She showed me where to stroke behind the ears, and I snuggled my nose into its sweet fur. "Feel anything?" She asked.

"Love and warm rainbows."

She smiled. "No itchy nose?"

"Nothing."

"OK, come over here." She removed the bunny from my hands against my will and led me to a cage full of tiny brown and white rodents, short-snouted versions of Hammy. She reached in and selected one for me.

I held it up to my nose. Nothing. Damn! That was my whole theory up in smoke.

"Not allergic?"

"No, but I was positive I was." I hung my head.

Cindy and Darcy exchanged sly glances before bursting out laughing. Darcy delivered the punch line. "That's a hamster, not a gerbil!"

Oh, what fun. "Do you have gerbils?" I asked impatiently.

"Over here." Cindy led me two cages down, and my eyes started watering immediately. I wasn't even holding the gerbil when the sneezing began.

"Yup," Darcy said. "You're allergic."

Just to be sure, he handed me one. My eyeballs burned so bad they tried to scratch themselves, and the postnasal drip was immediate. I thanked them profusely and scurried out of the house.

Next stop, Gary Wohnt. Despite no longer being police chief, he had reclaimed his old office, making me wonder where Kennie had set up shop. He was sitting behind his imposing metal desk rifling through paperwork when I entered.

"Got a minute?"

He peered up, and I steeled myself. His glance left me bare, but this time I didn't fight it. He was in his deep blue uniform, hat off to reveal slicked-back black hair. Judging by the soft appearance of his mouth, I guessed he still had his Carmex habit, but his lips were the only soft thing on him. His face was chiseled, shoulders broad. I stood my ground and let him give me the up down. I was here for once not because I felt guilty but because I wanted to help him.

"One."

"That's all I need." I dragged the lone empty chair in the room to the front of his desk and laid into the story. I told him how I'd sneezed when I'd first come upon Webber's body. I hadn't thought much of it until I realized that I had the same reaction whenever I was near Kenya, who always kept her trained gerbil close at hand. And then, I pulled it all together with the coup de grace: gerbil turds found around Webber's body in a room that Kenya had no reason to be in if she wasn't killing Webber. I explained that although Kenya had provided an alibi for her mother the night of Webber's murder, she'd also said her mother had been knocked out on sleeping pills and so Kenya herself had no alibi. And I shared my fear that Kenya had given her mom sleeping pills and then killed her, too.

He held up his hand. And then held it there for a moment longer, apparently searching for the right words. "You're asking me to accuse a woman of two murders because you're allergic to her pet?"

"It's not a lot, I know, but she's unstable. Glokkmann told me Kenya has attachment disorder, and a symptom of that is defiance and inappropriate attachments. She had motive to kill Webber to frame her mom."

"A lot of people had motive," he said. His sleeves were rolled back enough to reveal muscled forearms flexing with impatience. "What makes you think she also killed her mother?"

"I didn't at first. I thought Glokkmann really had killed herself to protect her daughter—she'd told me in jail that she'd do anything for her kids—but then her assistant Grace told me at the funeral that the Representative would never have done that. And she's right. Glokkmann was selfish, superficial, and too convinced of her own worth to ever end her own life."

He glared at me wordlessly.

"Look," I said. "If you can prove her gerbil was in the room Webber was murdered in, wouldn't that be enough?"

"Not by a long shot." He steepled his fingers. "And the room has been thoroughly cleaned."

My heart sank. "I know I haven't always been up front with you, or reliable, but I know she did it, Gary. I know it."

I'd never called him by his first name before, and it hung in the air between us awkwardly. The muscles on his forearms flexed again. Finally, he spoke, his voice low and controlled. "What did you have in mind?"

"A sting."

His eyes flashed with impatience or suppressed laughter. I was not good at reading this man. "A sting?"

"Yes, a sting."

He arranged the papers on his desk, standing to file a loose one. I couldn't help but stare at his butt, which looked roughly firm enough to crack a walnut. Damn that man and his psy ops. He turned and caught me staring. A muscle in his cheek jumped, and he sat back down. "I'll pass on the sting. And if I hear that you're within a hundred yards of Kenya Glokkmann, I'll arrest you."

I coughed on my own spit. "On what charges?"

"Don't need any. At least not right away."

I was so angry I could only see out of one eye. "Is that all?"

"You tell me."

The one time in my life I needed a comeback more than a fish needed water, and I had nothing. I stormed out, slamming the door on my way and then returning to slam it again.

TWENTY-SEVEN

I WAS SO ANGRY when I stomped out of the police department that my footprints gave off sparks. Sure, the phrase "the gerbil turd" wasn't going to replace "the smoking gun" in the lexicon anytime soon, but Gary didn't seem to have anything better to go on. What a hardass he was. Literally, not figuratively, dammit.

But I didn't need him. I'd stumbled through by myself just fine until now. Well, sort of. The bummer was that if I was going to nail Kenya, I *did* need Bad Brad. I tromped over to his two-bedroom apartment above the Klassy Kwilt Shoppe in downtown Battle Lake and rang the bell.

He buzzed me in, informing me over the intercom that his apartment was the third door on my right at the top of the stairs. He was thrilled to see me, meeting me in the hallway and offering me a tour of his digs. I'd never been to his local abode before and followed him in reluctantly. I thought it a gimme that the place would be a dump with beer cases standing in for furniture and trash to the ceiling, but I found it to be neatly-kept. One of the bedrooms housed his musical instruments, all of them in their cases on a custom-built shelf or displayed on the wall. Peeking in the second bedroom revealed that the bedspread didn't match his pillow cases or his curtains, but he had all three, and they were where they should be. In his kitchen, his dishes had been washed and were drying, and he even had a (intentionally) dried flower bouquet on this kitchen table. The furniture in the living room was old and mismatched but there were no dirty clothes lying around or dust collecting. I refused to go into his bathroom for fear of finding that he did *not* have booby magazines stacked next to the toilet. That would be too much topsy-turviness for one day.

While Brad showed me around, I filled him in on the details of my plan. Part of me didn't want to tell him the whole story, that I thought Kenya had tricked Webber into meeting her in a room she knew would be empty so she could knock him out, suffocate him, string some of her mom's hair around his fingers, and stomp around in her mom's shoes, made muddy courtesy of the ditch and some lake water. I didn't know how to convince him to secure to his person the handheld tape recorder I'd picked up at the hardware store on the way over without telling him, though, and I certainly didn't know how I'd get him to trap her into confessing if he didn't have some insider info. Plus, it hurts to lie to a guy without eyebrows.

He was alarmingly happy to help. "I'm Crockett and you're Tubbs, dude!"

Before I even finished outlining the whole plan, he'd tossed some Phil Collins into his stereo and thrown a mint green blazer on over his worn Hüsker Dü T-shirt before racing to call Kenya. I had to push him down and remind him we needed Vanderbrick's assistance before we phoned her. Fortunately, Vanderbrick was home and happy to help after I explained what was going down.

That piece in place, I gave Brad the thumbs up to call the woman who'd been phoning him several times a day since their Octoberfest rendezvous. He pitched his voice low and invited her over to do the no-pants dance. He sure knew how to sweet talk the ladies. I heard him wheedle her, convince her that time away from her family would be the best thing for her tonight, and finally, she relented. He hung up the phone and said Kenya was almost done with her funeral obligations and would be here within the hour.

The final phase of the puzzle was for me to duct tape the portable tape recorder to Brad's body. When he pulled up his shirt, I shouldn't have been surprised to see that he was shaved as clean as a volleyball.

"The doctor do that?"

"Nope," he said, grinning happily. "In the Air Tonight" was weaving its way out of the speakers.

I refused to comment further. Once Brad was wired, I checked his computer for the millionth time to see if Vanderbrick had followed through. He'd been surprised to hear from me again, even more surprised when I explained that I thought Glokkmann's daughter had murdered Webber and then her mother. I promised to share all the details if he'd helped me. He said it wouldn't be easy, but he'd try his best. He still hadn't fulfilled his end of the bargain, though.

Brad offered to sing a love song for me to pass the time. When I declined, he asked if I'd like to play his skin flute. I also took a pass on that. And Vanderbrick still hadn't come through. If he didn't or couldn't stick to his word, this plan was sunk and Kenya would walk away from two murders. The clock told me she'd be here in less than fifteen minutes, and still nothing.

"Maybe you should restart the computer. It's pretty old."

I took Brad's advice for the first and last time and was almost disappointed that it worked. Vanderbrick had written and posted the article just like he'd said he would, with only five minutes until Kenya's ETA. Leaving the screen up and sequestering myself into the closet off the living room, I realized I felt sorry for both of today's main actors. There was Brad, who kept his house clean but had so thoroughly bought into his own myth that he couldn't be a decent person for more than thirty seconds in a row, and Kenya, who had apparently suffered so much when she was just a toddler or at the hands of her verbally vicious mother that she'd matured into a killer.

I pushed those thoughts away and settled back just in time, leaving a slight crack in the door. The doorbell rang, a pleasant inhale-exhale of a chime. Brad flipped up his collar and tossed thumbs up back at me.

"Stop it," I hissed. "Remember, I'm not here."

He sang a couple bars of "Easy Lover" before opening the door. I couldn't believe he was still thinking he'd see some action. If I was right, Kenya was as balanced as a corporate checkbook, and Brad was putting himself in deep danger by inviting her here.

"Baby!" That's all Brad had time to say before Kenya jumped in the air and wrapped her legs around him, kissing his face like a honey bear and stroking the arms of his pastel blazer.

I leaned back from the crack in the door, my eye burning. Was I willing to listen to Brad and Kenya going at it in the off chance that she'd confess at some point? That's when an icy reminder pushed my face back to the crack. If she kept stroking his body like she was trying to shine her silver, she'd find the sleek voice recorder taped between his shoulder blades. He must have remembered the same thing, because he pulled her away from him and tossed her on the couch, out of my line of sight.

"What's wrong?" She asked. I could tell from the high tone of her voice that she was worked up.

"Nothing, sweetcakes! I just like a little anticipation." I caught a glimpse of him striding toward the computer.

"That's not what you said when you invited me here. You said you were going to make love to me. That's why I came. I missed you, Brad." She lunged off the couch and also passed across my line of sight.

"I've missed you too, baby, I really have, and I want to make this special. Can I get you some wine?"

She giggled and then bounced back past the couch and into the kitchen. Brad followed. I heard the clinking of glasses and the throaty, insider laughter of two people dancing the pre-sex polka. It was driving me crazy, not hearing what they were saying, and I wanted to crack the door wider to improve my amplification. But I didn't, fortunately, as they returned to the sofa moments later.

I heard the squeak of couch springs and the rustle of clothing. "I've been worried about you, baby."

"You've got a big heart." I sensed she was reaching for a part of him that definitely wasn't his heart, though it probably had a comparable blood supply.

"That can wait. I wanna talk first."

My heart was thumping so loudly it echoed off the walls of the closet. This was the moment. This segue is exactly what we'd talked about. He'd been certain she'd show up raring for action. The plan was that he'd lead her on and prime her with wine. When her guard was down he'd spill about the blog entry he'd "found." What happened next relied completely on his ability to convince her that he regularly followed *The Body Politic*. It was the weakest link in our otherwise anemic plan.

"I've got something much more fun that I want to do with my mouth." I heard the jangle of wine glasses being set down and the wet friction of kissing followed by the crisp whip of a zipper being opened.

"I wanna talk now," Brad said, his voice husky. He stood and positioned himself in my line of sight, his side to me. Kenya followed, leaning against his shoulder, her face toward me. Her gaze was so intense that I was certain she could see me. He pulled up his zipper.

And that's when I saw it. It was a switch, an audible click, an eerie shift as clear as white against black. Her face, next to his ear, had gone psychoceramic. "You didn't want to talk when I was calling you every day," she rasped dangerously.

Brad was oblivious to Kenya's unhinging. "That was then, this is now, baby. I've got something I have to tell you. You know that guy who was murdered here last week? I was reading his blog. You know, curious who he was since he was killed just up the road. Anyway, he posted something the night he was murdered, and I think you wanna see it."

Brad disappeared from my sight and must have strolled toward his computer. He didn't see the black-ice stare Kenya gave his back, but I did, and it made my stomach gurgle. She wasn't all there anymore. Some bedrock part of her had fled. I wanted to stand, to stop what I knew was unfolding, but it was like I was watching a distant play.

"It's about you." Brad kept his voice surprised and sincere. "He wrote that you asked him to meet in his friend's empty room that Saturday night but weren't there when he showed up. You were going to give him some information about your mom that would ruin her. But you didn't show when you said you would, so he went back to his room to type up his blog post. The last thing he wrote was that you had called and he was going to meet you in room 19 for sure this time."

We were winging this last part. When I'd crossed paths with Webber on the motel stairs last Saturday, he'd been agitated. I had an inkling that was because Kenya had originally stood him up. If true, it was a detail that only she and Webber would have known, and it would have to be enough to convince her that the blog post Vanderbrick had just posted on Webber's site was genuine.

"I know you met him there later, and you killed him, and I'm glad you did, baby. He was a prick. An absolute prick."

All the air in the room grew heavy and dropped to the ground, making it difficult to breathe. I was sure Brad had overplayed his hand. Kenya was as still as rock, her eyes black and wide, her mouth a stiff red slash across her face. She was either going to laugh in his face or slice it off and eat his nose with a dessert fork. "He wasn't. He wasn't a bad man at all."

"What?" Her voice was soft, and Brad, who I could hear still fooling with his computer, didn't hear her the first time.

"I was just going to tell him how he was right, and my mom was an alcoholic, and she did take bribes. I had the evidence, and I could have just handed it to him. But she would have squirmed her way out of that. She walked away clean from everything. And so he died. Hammy helped me." She laughed, and it sounded like wind through a skull.

"Hammy?"

She reached onto the table behind her for her purse, and then a puzzled look crossed her face, quickly replaced by a serene smile. "He's my gerbil. He's not here."

"He helped you to suffocate Webber? That's what I don't get. I don't get how a little thing like you could kill a guy." Brad was talking fast, and I could tell he was beginning to feel anxious.

"I gave him one of my mom's sleeping pills, all crushed up in wine. It made him slow. When his back was to me, I hit him with a hotel chair. That didn't kill him, so I took the bag out of the bathroom garbage and tied it around his neck. Shooting the Queen was even easier."

Brad's voice shook. "Well, it's done, and that's what's important." Not as important as me spending the extra $1.23 on the 90-minute tape, apparently, because that's when it ran out. The record button popped out as loudly as a firecracker.

Kenya jumped, startled. "What was that?"

Brad attempted a clicking sound in his throat. "Beatboxing. A new thing for the band. You like?" He continued to wheeze and chirrup like a tractor straining up a hill.

She shook her head slowly and held her arms out, her purse still clutched in one hand. "Come hold me."

God save him, Brad did. Now they were both in my line of sight. She wrapped her arms around him and dipped her head into his chest. "I'm guilty," she whispered. "I did it. I killed Webber and I shot my mom."

Brad laughed uncomfortably but didn't push her away. Her purse fell to the ground, and in her hand and behind his back was a gun. I choked.

"We could go out like Thelma and Louise," she sighed, slowly raising the barrel of the pistol to the back of his neck.

I powered through my fear and yelled. Kenya staggered back and pointed the gun toward the closet door. Without time to think, I stood and pushed it open and found myself staring into the bottomless black barrel of her pistol. The whole scene felt slow-moving and ridiculous, way more watery and surreal than in the movies. It didn't have to end this way. But Kenya's eyes were lit by crazy, and the three

215

of us were not walking out of here. Her finger clenched against the trigger. Brad whimpered but didn't move. This must have felt as inevitable to him as it did to me.

And then the front door exploded.

TWENTY-EIGHT

"Everybody down!"

Deputy Wohnt led the charge but two plainclothes officers were directly on his heels. I was still partially in the closet and obliged immediately with the command. Brad also dropped to the ground and then scurried past me so he was fully in the closet.

Kenya did not respond. She studied the three men, guns drawn, their breath coming in adrenaline bursts, exactly like she'd studied me the first time we'd met at the side of the stage on debate day. She was a hawk, recording every detail before deciding whether they were worth her attention. Her gun had been hanging at her side but she drew it slowly up, swiveling the end toward her face. I lunged forward to grab it, but Wohnt was quicker. He fired a single shot at her right shoulder and she dropped her weapon and crumpled.

One of the officers moved swiftly to retrieve the pistol and the other called for an ambulance on his shoulder unit.

"Are you okay?"

Wohnt had crossed the room in three strides. He made a move to reach toward me but stopped abruptly, turning back to focus on Kenya. He flipped her over. Her eyes were open and she was shivering. There wasn't much blood, even when he ripped her shirt open to get a clear look at the wound. "I need a blanket and a clean towel."

I followed his orders as best I could. My legs were shaky but they carried me into Brad's bedroom and then bathroom. I was distantly relieved to see the latest issue of *Juggz and Huggz* on the sink next to his toilet. I hurried back and handed Wohnt the cloth. He staunched Kenya's wound and covered her with the blanket. When the paramedics arrived moments later, some color had returned to her cheeks.

They hauled her out, and Wohnt and the remaining officer stayed behind. Wohnt turned to me, fire blazing in his eyes. He shoved me onto the couch and stood over me. "This the sting?"

At first I couldn't meet his gaze, adrenaline and shock swirling dangerously fast in my stomach. Then I remembered that discomfort and indignation were close cousins and I shot to my feet, jabbing him in the chest with my finger. "I asked for your help but you weren't interested. Said my gerbil turd theory was stupid. Said that wasn't enough to go on." I walked angrily toward the closet, knocking Wohnt out of the way. I leaned forward and snaked my arm down the back of still-cowering Brad's shirt. A loud ripping sound followed by a sad squeal from Brad, and I had the tape recorder in hand. "Here. Why don't you see if that's enough to go on."

Wohnt's eyes were glittering dangerously. "What will I hear if I listen to this?"

"Kenya confessing to killing Webber. And her mother."

The other officer came up behind Gary and clapped him on the shoulder. "You were right about her."

They exchanged a look, and I couldn't read either damn one of their faces. Hysteria and rage vied for position in my cluttered head. "Right about what? Right that you should listen to me more? Right that I was right and you were wrong?"

My voice went a little screechy as the reality of what had just happened closed over me. "Right that all the men in my life are either too good for me, dead, or fiberglass statues?"

"I'm not too good for you!" Brad said from the closet.

"Shut up." I shoved my hands on my hips. "Right that you can get me to confess to Watergate with that cop stare of yours, and that I'm an eyelash shy of a nervous breakdown and that I would have been better off moving to Siberia than Battle Lake and that I'm going to die a lonely old cat lady?"

Gary was vibrating ever so slightly, and I thought he was going to yell at me before I realized he was laughing.

His back-up shook his head in wonder. "Yup, absolutely right."

TWENTY-NINE

"I THINK HE MEANT that Wohnt was right that you're about as lucky as a three-legged cat," said Mrs. Berns.

"What does that even mean?" I couldn't believe how lovely she looked in the white wedding gown. It was two weeks since her car accident, and although the bruises on her face had faded to the color of dirt smudges and she was still crutch-bound, she glowed. The dress was shamelessly white and flowing and fitted at the top to display more cleavage than I'd ever seen on her. As her matron of honor, something she insisted on calling me given what she referred to as my "geriatric" sex life, I was at the Senior Sunset curling her hair and helping her with her makeup. I didn't know how to do either so she mostly shooed me away and took care of business herself, as usual. She insisted I fill her in on every speck of what she referred to as the "Gerbil Turd Sting."

"I don't know. Tell me again what you spewed toward the end?"

I told her. It didn't get better in the telling.

"Ah. I retract my first answer. My best guess is that Wohnt has been telling people that you're a nice girl who needs to get laid in the worst way."

"Nobody *needs* to get laid."

"Speak for yourself."

I wasn't going to argue. She was the expert at this table. I indicated the front of her dress. "Where've you been hiding those boobs, anyway?"

"When you get to be my age, you just roll 'em up. Your cups runneth over even if it takes a while to locate your nipples." She dusted glittery powder over her soft and wrinkled skin. "So you didn't finish your story. What's going to happen to that crazy girl Africa now that you got her confession on tape?"

"Kenya. And since she confessed again to killing Webber and her mom on the way to the hospital, I think she's going away for good. Her dad's found her a good lawyer, though, so you never know."

"She say why she did it?"

I shook my head. "Not really. Just that she hated her mom and wasn't going to let her continue to ruin lives."

Mrs. Berns tsked. "Makes my kids look like angels for only wanting to incarcerate me in a maximum security nursing home."

"Not kids, kid. Just Conrad. Remember that Elizabeth is on your team now." I studied my fingernails. "You know what? When I think back to my conversation with Glokkmann at the jail, I think she knew Kenya had killed Webber and was hoping she would come forward on her own. Guess that wasn't her best gamble."

"I'll say. I've been meaning to mention, you get all glowy when you talk about solving crimes. You ever notice that?"

I had. "Is it weird?"

"If you mean is it uncommon, most good things are. You ever thought about going pro?"

"What do you mean?"

"I mean this." She pulled open the top drawer of her vanity and handed me a stack of papers from the Minnesota Private Detective and Protective Agent Licensing Board.

Just reading the letterhead made me shiver, in a good way, but I played it cool. "I don't know."

"Sure you do."

She was right. I smiled and hugged her. "You wanna do the training with me?"

"Maybe. Depends how much work it is."

"Thank you," I said. "Thank you, thank you! You know you're my best friend, right?"

"I better be. I made you my matron of honor." She liked calling me that.

I stuffed the papers into my purse. I'd have to read them later, when the idea of becoming a private investigator didn't seem so big and intimidating. Besides, tonight was all about Mrs. Berns. "Are all your kids invited to the wedding?"

"Can't remember." Her voice had taken an ornery cast. "Say, did I tell you that the kitchen staff here cooked up your Eerie Ground Liver Pie for supper at the Sunset last night? That's gotta be your best recipe yet. How'd you think of adding salted peanuts?"

I shrugged. "Creating gross food is my gift to share with the world. So you're really going through with this?" The ceremony was scheduled to begin at seven o'clock, and her friends had gone on ahead to adorn the church with votives so Mrs. Berns could have the candlelit wedding of her dreams. Outside, groups of ghouls and zombies were traveling door-to-door, filling their bags with enough candy to make stomachs hurt for months. Long live sugar-based socialism.

"I'm wearing the dress, ain't I?"

"You sure are," I said. "You look beautiful." She really did. Her hair was curled and her eyes were bright. She had lovely deep lines on her face from smiling and cracking wise.

"And I'm not getting any younger. Time to hit the road."

I helped her up and to the car and drove the short distance to Trinity Lutheran. My heart was heavy. Bernard was more of a dink than a Mink, but she'd chosen him as the best candidate to guard her future until Conrad decided to leave her alone. I didn't think it was a good idea, but I didn't have the threat of a maximum security nursing home hanging over my head. I had to support her as a friend. She'd still find a way to be Mrs. Berns, even within the temporary confines of marriage.

Outside the church, glimmering jack-o-lanterns lit the steps all the way to the heavy wooden doors, and I smiled. Yes, she would always find a way to be Mrs. Berns. As I got out of the car to help her, I heard the organ version of "Thriller" filtering out from the closed church doors. I navigated Mrs. Berns' wedding train and crutches so she could lean on me to limp up the stairs.

Inside, the church was full, beaming faces turning to take in the blushing bride. Half the town must have been in attendance. The interior of the church was magical, with the tiny teardrops of hundreds of yellow flames glinting off of the stained glass and illuminating the gold and white ribbons twining along the edges of the pews. The heady perfume of white roses floated on the air. Bernard was nowhere in sight.

Framed by the open church doors, Mrs. Berns smacked her crutch against the floor three times, like a gavel. "I have an announcement to make!" Her voice rang out, the organ stopped, and those few who had missed her entrance turned. I wondered what was up. We hadn't discussed this.

"First things first. I need to speak to my children. All of you, front and center."

Eight people stood and walked toward their mother, who looked imposing, even on crutches. Every one of them sported the hatchet nose they must have inherited from their father. They were dressed formally.

"Conrad here wants to send me to prison camp. Who else is on board with him?"

The church crowd booed.

"Mother, this isn't the time," Conrad began.

"It's the only time I'll get all eight of you in a room together. Lord knows you don't visit on the holidays. Now, who's on Conrad's team and who's on mine?"

Seven of them gathered around her, leaving Conrad standing alone. Whispers ran along the edge of the church as people craned their necks to view the outcome.

"I'm on your team, mother." Conrad's arms hung stiffly at his side even as his voice entreated her. "That's why I'm trying to take care of you."

"Conrad Berns, you listen to me good because I'm only going to say this once. I spent the first twenty years of my life taking care of my brothers and sisters, the next thirty taking care of my ungrateful kids, and the twenty-odd after that taking care of my husband and parents. For the first time in my life, I'm taking care of myself. I plan to make some mistakes, but it's not your job to take care of me, it's mine. *Comprende vu?*"

He tried to stare her down, but she didn't back off. "You're not going to listen to me no matter what, are you?" he asked.

"Ah, so you're not a complete idiot."

"Fine, mother." His shoulders slumped and he looked for all the world like a sullen little boy.

"Not yet, it isn't. You're going to apologize to me in front of all these people, and you and the kids are going to all promise, out loud, that you're never going to try to get me declared legally incompetent again."

Conrad looked ready to protest, but the angry murmurings of the crowd silenced him. All eight children agreed that Mrs. Berns was capable of making her own decisions.

"Now it's fine!" She said triumphantly. "Time to party! Let's go." And she turned toward the door.

Out of the corner of my eye, I finally spotted a nervous-looking Bernard off to my right. He was wearing a cheap tux over a ruffled blue dress shirt. He appeared to be trying to slink out a side door, but there was a firm hand on his arm, attached to a lean, hard body that went by the name of Johnny Leeson. Johnny's face was grim but he flashed me a quick smile that made me shiver.

I broke eye contact and whispered to Mrs. Berns. "You haven't gotten hitched yet."

"Duh. I wasn't ever going to go through with it. I just needed my kids off my back and an excuse to party. Oh, and a chance to humiliate Bernard in public. The guy's a jackass."

Tanya Ingebretson, who was sitting in the back row with her husband, gasped. "But we talked about this in great detail! This is a major step in your remodeling. The wedding will transform you."

"Same me, better dress. And your life coaching? I've gotten better advice from a Magic 8 Ball. But thanks for keeping my kids off my back long enough to get them all together."

Tanya gasped again, but Mrs. Berns' attention had already moved elsewhere. "Off to the Rusty Nail! First round's on me. I have the kids' inheritance to spend." She cackled and cleared a path with her crutches before limping out.

I raced to catch up with her, my heart light. Behind us was the sound of a couple hundred people gathering their belongings. "So you were never going to go through with it?"

"Please. Have you even looked at Bernard? He might know his way around a bedroom but he's a musty old thing, and bossy to boot. Stupid enough to think he's in charge, and that's the only good thing I can say about him."

"I'm right here," he whined, appearing at her side. "Where's my money?"

"If it was up your butt, you'd know."

He wasn't smiling. "Five thousand dollars. That's what we agreed on."

"I was double undercover, Bernard. I lied to my kids about getting married to keep them off my back, but I had to also make you believe we were actually going through with it and that I'd pay you or you'd never have stuck around long enough to get everyone in this church. And don't think I didn't see you trying to sneak out just now when you thought this was going down."

"But we had a deal," he griped.

"I've already paid you more than you're worth, Bernard. I put up with your attitude, broke my ribs and leg because of you, and I got Mira here to clear your name in a murder investigation so I didn't have to hire another patsy to play my fiancé. I think *you* owe *me* money."

I stepped in. "Scram, Bernard. She knows how to use those crutches, and I've seen her drop a man twice your size. She knows where to grab."

He looked ready to put up a fight, but a couple of Battle Lake's bigger, kinder brutes materialized from the crowd, catching scent of Mrs. Berns in trouble. Bernard might be stupid, but he wasn't dumb, and he stomped off. I had a feeling we hadn't seen the last of him, but I was too ecstatic to care too much right now—Mrs. Berns wasn't getting married!

We were at my car. I eased her into the passenger seat and tucked her crutches in back, unable to wipe the smile off my face. Around us, people were talking and laughing, many of them taking advantage of the unseasonably warm fall evening to walk to the Rusty Nail. I noticed none of them had gifts. I looked to Mrs. Berns suspiciously. "Was I the only one who didn't know this was a fake wedding?"

"Maybe, if you don't count my kids and Bernard," she said. "But Lord knows you can't keep a secret, and I needed my kids to believe there was going to be a real wedding." She pinched my arm. "Looks like someone wants to talk to you."

I turned. Johnny stood at the top of the church steps, leaning against the open door. The wind ruffled his curling dirty blond hair, and he had a faint grin playing on his lips. He'd undone his tie and his crisp white dress shirt was open at the collar. I could make out a hint of his muscled chest, and his pleated slacks fit him like a hand to a glove. I wondered idly if I could get him to put on a loincloth and hold a tomahawk in an erect position.

"I've given up on men," I managed to choke out. "I'm going to be single forever."

"Get off that egg," Mrs. Berns said. "You don't have the stones for it. You know you want him."

She was right. I offered him a timid smile. His grin grew. He pushed off the door and sauntered down the steps toward me. He was sexy-on-a-stick, open and loving, and I wanted those lean hips against mine until I screamed out for more.

I heard Mrs. Berns shift in the car and chuckle. "I think tonight's going to be a night to remember."

"I'm scared," I said, as Johnny neared.

She grabbed my hand and said just loud enough for me to hear, "It's tough sometimes, Mira James, but when life squeezes you, you gotta trust your own juice."

"Yeah," I said, stepping forward and into Johnny's arms. "I just might try that."

DISCUSSION QUESTIONS

1. Mira is feeling more jaded in her Battle Lake experience, and that's coming through in her voice. Do you think she should stay, or return to Minneapolis to finish her graduate degree in English?

2. Gary Wohnt is evolving in this book. What role do you see him taking in the series in the future?

3. Some people believe politics and mysteries should never mix. What are the pros and cons of having political characters in a humorous mystery series?

4. Mira often feels like a fish out of water navigating the rules of the small town. Can you identify with the strains she experiences? Along those same lines, which is the better place to live—a city or a small town?

5. Is Johnny really the perfect guy? Or does he have some skeletons in his closet? Will Mira ever get over her awkward behavior with him?

6. Do mysteries have to have the resolution of bad guy being caught, girl gets the guy, all's right with the world? Can the bad guy get away and the girl be alone and broken-hearted?

7. Is the series growing slightly more serious? Does that make it more or less interesting?

8. What do you think of Kennie Rogers' latest money-making scheme? Who is the most outrageous character, Kennie or Mrs. Berns?

Jane Bailey Photography, Inc.

ABOUT THE AUTHOR

Jess Lourey spent her formative years in Paynesville, Minnesota, a small town not unlike the Murder-by-Month series' Battle Lake. She teaches English and sociology full time at a two-year college. When not raising her wonderful kids, teaching, or writing, you can find her gardening and navigating the niceties and meanities of small-town life. She is a member of Mystery Writers of America, Sisters in Crime, the Loft, and Lake Superior Writers.